sweet dreams

sweet dreams

a novel

Massimo Gramellini

Translated by Stephen Parkin

ATRIA PAPERBACK

New York   London   Toronto   Sydney   New Delhi

ATRIA PAPERBACK

A Division of Simon & Schuster, Inc.
1230 Avenue of the Americas
New York, NY 10020

Copyright © 2012 by Massimo Gramellini
English language translation © 2014 by Stephen Parkin
Published by arrangement with Alma Books Ltd
First published in Italian as *Fai bei sogni* by Longanesi & C., Gruppo editoriali Mauri Spagnol, in 2012

First Atria Paperback edition April 2014

ATRIA PAPERBACK and colophon are trademarks of Simon & Schuster, Inc.

For information about special discounts for bulk purchases, please contact Simon & Schuster Special Sales at 1-866-506-1949 or business@simonandschuster.com.

The Simon & Schuster Speakers Bureau can bring authors to your live event. For more information or to book an event, contact the Simon & Schuster Speakers Bureau at 1-866-248-3049 or visit our website at www.simonspeakers.com.

Interior design by Leydiana Rodríguez-Ovalles
Cover design by Zoe Norvell
Cover art by Marko Mastosaari

Manufactured in the United States of America

10   9   8   7   6   5   4   3   2   1

Library of Congress Cataloging-in-Publication Data has been applied for.

ISBN 978-1-4767-1860-6
ISBN 978-1-4767-1861-3 (ebook)

To my mother,

Giuseppina Pastore

Far more important than what
we know or do not know is
what we do not want to know.

—Eric Hoffer

sweet dreams

On New Year's eve, like every year, I called on my god-mother to take her to see Mom.

My godmother is a piece of antique furniture in a very good state of conservation. She lives on her own in a house filled with sunlight, where she spends her time reading detective novels and chatting to the framed photographs of her husband. Occasionally she changes shelf and talks to the photograph of Mom, mostly about me.

I imagine she omits the more unwelcome news. Such as the fact I've had two wives—though not, it's true, at the same time. And that I never did become a lawyer.

While I was helping her into her coat, she brought up the subject of the novel I had given her for Christmas.

"I finished it last night."

"Did you enjoy it? It's not a detective novel."

"Of course I did: you wrote it."

"And the passages about Mom?"

"That's the part I wanted to talk to you about."

"It's the only part which is autobiographical. I put a bit of the story of my own life into those pages."

"Are you sure it's your story?"

"And why wouldn't it be?"

"It wasn't exactly like that . . . I want to give you something, dear."

I watched her fumble with dwarf-sized keys at the drawers of the bureau. Her lovely, gnarled old hands drew out a brown envelope. She handed it to me with a quivering voice: "After forty years, it's time that someone told you the truth."

forty years earlier

one

Forty years earlier, on New Year's Eve, I woke up so early I thought I was still dreaming. I remember the scent of my mother in my room and her dressing gown at the foot of the bed. What was it doing there?

And then the snow on the window sill, the lights all on throughout the house, a sound of feet dragging along and that howl, like some wounded animal:

"Nooooo!"

I pushed my slippers onto the wrong feet, but there was no time to correct the mistake. The door was already creaking open as I pushed it with my hands, until I saw him in the middle of the hallway, next to the Christmas tree—Daddy.

The great oak tree I looked up to as a child, bent

double like a willow by some invisible force, with a pair of strangers holding him up under the arms.

He was wearing the purple dressing gown my mother had given him—the one held together with a curtain cord instead of a belt. He jerked about, kicking and twisting.

As soon as he saw I was there, I heard him murmur: "He's my son . . . Please, take him over to the neighbors'."

His head fell backwards and bumped against the Christmas tree. An angel with glass wings lost its balance and toppled to the floor.

The two strangers didn't speak, but they were kind, and they left me with Tiglio and Palmira, an elderly married couple who lived in the flat on the opposite side of the landing.

Tiglio faced life armed in the striped pajamas he always wore and comforted by a stubborn deafness. He communicated only in writing, but that morning he refused to reply to the questions I scrawled in block letters in the margins of the newspaper

WHERE'S
MOMMY?
HAS DADDY
BEEN
ROBBED?

Thieves must have got in during the night . . . perhaps they were the two men who'd been holding him by the arms?

Palmira came in with the shopping.

"Your daddy had a bit of a headache. He's all right now. Those two men were the doctors who came to see him."

"Why didn't they have white coats on?"

"They only put them on when they're in the hospital."

"Why were there two of them?"

"The emergency doctors always go around in pairs."

"I see—so if one of them feels ill the other one can look after him. Where's Mommy?"

"Daddy's gone out with her. They had something to do."

"When is she coming back?"

"She'll be back soon, you'll see. Do you want a cup of hot chocolate?"

In the absence of my mother, I made do with the chocolate.

———

A few hours later Giorgio and Ginetta, my parents' best friends, came to take charge of me.

I'm not sure I ever thought of them as two separate people. My parents had met at their wedding, a circumstance which never failed to set my little head whirring.

"Mommy, if Giorgio and Ginetta had forgotten to take you to their wedding, would you still be my mommy or someone else who was there?"

Even though it was patched and torn like a workman's overalls, my tongue was never still.

"It's a miracle with a tongue in that condition your son can speak," the pediatrician had told my mother.

"It would be a miracle if I could get him to be quiet every now and then, Doctor," my mother had replied. "He talks nonstop . . . he'll end up becoming a lawyer."

I didn't agree. I wanted to stop talking and start writing instead. Whenever I felt some adult had been unfair towards me, I would shake a pen in their face: "When I'm grown up, I'll write it all down in a book called *Me as a Child.*"

The title could be improved, but the book itself would be explosive.

The truth was I would have preferred to be a painter. By the age of six I had already painted my last masterpiece: *Mommy Eating a Bunch of Grapes*. The bunch was twice the size of my mother, the grapes looked like the baubles on a Christmas tree, and my mother's face resembled a grape.

She had put it up in the kitchen and would proudly point it out to visiting relatives. Seeing the puzzled looks on their faces, life dealt me its first blow: I was never going to succeed as a painter. I would have to try to draw the world inside me in words.

———————

Back in Giorgio and Ginetta's home, the saddest New Year's Eve dinner ever took place. Despite my efforts to enliven the conversation, their thirteen-year-old son and myself were hurried off to our bunk beds at nine o'clock, after a bowl of pasta and a veal cutlet, both cooked in butter.

There was no way of getting a slice of panettone or a decent explanation out of them. Mommy and Daddy had something to do—perhaps the same thing they'd had to do in the morning or perhaps something else, but equally mysterious. And we boys had to head for the Land of Nod as fast as our legs would carry us.

I remember the regular breathing of my cellmate in the bunk above me. And the fireworks at midnight, which stained the dark of the room through the only partly lowered blinds.

Buried beneath the blankets, my eyes wide open and

my head in a whirl like some top which couldn't stop spinning, I kept asking myself what I could possibly have done during the Christmas holidays to deserve a punishment like this.

I'd told two fibs, answered my mother back once and given Riccardo, the boy from the second floor who was a Juventus supporter, a kick in the backside. None of them seemed to me like capital offenses—especially the last.

two

On New Year's Day, Giorgio and Ginetta told me that when she'd returned from doing her errands my mother had had to go to hospital for a few tests. The last few months had been full of things she'd had to do and tests she'd had to take. Tests in hospital that is: if she'd come to school with me, I could have shown her how to copy the answers.

I imagined her tackling one of the problems our teacher had set us for the holidays. A little boy walks three kilometers and every two hectometers he drops two balls: how many balls will he drop after 1,900 meters?

I hated that word—hectometers—just as I hated that stupid little boy who kept dropping balls all over the place and yet went on walking as if nothing had happened.

In the afternoon my father reappeared to take me to

the hospital to see my mother. He'd gone back to being an oak tree.

"Let's buy her some flowers first," I suggested.

"No. Let's first go and see Baloo. He needs to tell you something important."

I dug my heels in. Baloo was the priest who ran the local Cubs, which I'd been going to for some months. I didn't mind saying hello to him, but he should wait his turn, instead of cutting in front of my mother.

Giorgio and Ginetta intervened and proposed an honorable compromise: we would still visit the hospital after we'd called on Baloo, but we would go and buy the flowers first.

————

I turned up at the church hall used by the Scouts holding an entire garden's worth of red roses in my arms.

Baloo had the same physical clumsiness and goodness of heart as his namesake in the *Jungle Book*. He took us into the Cubs' meeting room and straightaway cracked a joke about football. Even though he'd been born in Buenos Aires and lived in Turin like us, he was a fan of Cagliari and their star player Gigi Riva.

He wanted to show me some Panini cards of foot-ballers, but Dad stopped him.

"Show him another time, Baloo."

He gave a sigh and asked me to look up at the ceiling: a heaven of blue chalk drawings which I had helped to color in. Baloo plonked his huge hand down on my shoulder while pointing at the ceiling with the other.

"You know your mommy is your guardian angel, don't you? For a long time she's wanted to fly up there so she can look after you better—and yesterday the Lord called her to join him . . ."

An icy spoon turned in my stomach and hollowed it out. I spun round to my father, looking for some hint of a denial, but all I saw was his red eyes and pale lips.

"Let's go and pray," said Baloo.

———

"Eternal rest grant unto her, O Lord. Let perpetual light shine upon her. May she rest in peace. Amen."

Baloo's warm voice echoed through the nave of the empty church.

On my knees in the front pew, clasping the mass of red roses tightly to my chest, I moved my lips in time to his, but the words welling up from my heart were different. "Lord, give Mommy a short rest. Wake her up, make her some coffee and then send her back to me immediately . . . She's my mommy, so either bring her back here or take me up there. Please hurry up and choose. I'll close my eyes, and when I open them promise me you'll have made up your mind, all right? Amen."

three

My mother was laid out in the sitting room on view to the curious glances of the grieving neighbors.

I refused to go and look at her. I was sure she would come back. It's not in my nature to accept defeat. In the films I like best, the hero loses everything, but then, stepping away from the brink of the abyss, he begins his comeback.

Only as an adult would I learn not to shun open coffins. I'd also learn that the dead get smaller, almost as if their clothing of bones shrinks a couple of sizes when the spirit no longer fills it.

The dead grow smaller and the survivors turn sour like rejected lovers. They take offense when they see the world doesn't share their grief.

My grief made me impossible to deal with. It had happened two years before when I'd come round from an operation to remove my tonsils with my throat on fire and shouted at the doctors and relatives crowding round my bed: "Go away, all of you, I only want Mommy!"

This time I directed my snarls at the visitors to the apartment. But far from annoying them, my rudeness only made them even more keen to show their pity.

I couldn't bear their faces put on for the occasion, the compassionate caresses, the stupid phrases drifting through the room.

What a tragedy.

She was so young.

Poor little boy.

It's a terrible thing to get.

As if you could get a pleasant thing, one which did you the favour of leaving you alive.

———

Tonsillitis must have been a very pleasant thing then. During the weeks I was convalescing, I had no school homework to do, Mommy brought me ice creams and I was free to enjoy my secret hideaway, the Submarine.

At a certain point in the afternoon I would lower the

blinds and get back into bed with my head at the bottom and my feet under the pillow.

I would usually plunge down on my own, but on the trickier missions I got Nemecsek to come along with me. He was one of the Paul Street boys—the one who, even when he was dying, still dragged himself out of bed to go and help his companions in the decisive battle. The page was all tearstained in the book my mother had read to me.

Enemies encircled the Submarine on all sides but, protected by the magic bedsheet, I held out against their attacks until it was teatime and my mother came in with the tray. The fantasy gave me a feeling of security I've only found, since then, in the act of writing.

On the morning of the funeral I shut myself in my room and waited for the coffin to be taken out of the house. I lowered the blinds, got into bed head downwards and climbed aboard the Submarine wanting to declare war on the entire world. But there were no longer any enemies out there to be found: they were all inside me.

four

I started to hate her because she didn't come back. I tried
not to think about her, but hard as I might my thoughts
would automatically take over whenever I was tired, and
I would drift off into memories—the taste of the veal cut-
lets she used to cook in butter, the pleasant smell of her
hair whenever I gave her a hug, the last time we'd been
happy together.

They'd been showing an adaptation of the *Odyssey*
on the television and I'd been transfixed by the sight
of the cyclops Polyphemus flinging Ulysses's companions against the walls of his cave and then popping
them into his mouth like chips.

I imagined Polyphemus's voice to be harsh and alarm-
ing like that of the narrator of the series, the poet Giuseppe

Ungaretti. He was heard at the beginning of each episode reciting Homer's verses. As soon as his grating tones died away, a montage from previous episodes was shown summing up the story so far—which meant that the following week I again saw the scene with Polyphemus munching away.

Today's children are inured to scenes of killing and bloodshed on the television screen and would doubtless regard Polyphemus's grisly meal as a light snack. But I started to wake up in the middle of the night feeling like a particularly appetizing chip Polyphemus's single eye had greedily caught sight of. After putting up a brief struggle against the darkness I would give up and go and take refuge in my parents' bed.

In order to put a stop to these nightly migrations—I was, after all, a manly eight-year-old—my mother put an energy-saving night-light on my bedside table. Even so, we all knew another sight of the Cyclops would prove fatal.

On the evening of the final episode, just before the summary montage started to be shown, I fled into the kitchen with my mother, holding her tight, my nose in her blond hair—until my father, stationed by the TV set in the sitting room, gave the all-clear.

———

My other memories of her were confused and unsuppress-
ible, and tended to merge with more recent ones. When
had she stopped loving me? The light in those blue eyes
everyone knew had dimmed after the end of summer.
She'd suddenly turned fretful and gloomy. She'd always
had a smile for everyone, but it was plain her supply of
smiles had been used up.

One morning she wasn't there—she'd had to go and
"do something." A few days later she came back, even
sadder than before. Dad and I divided up our tasks: he
caressed her with words and I spoke to her with caresses.
But she didn't respond to either.

My godmother was her closest friend, and every
Sunday she and her husband, Uncle Nevio, would come
and visit us.

I would show off in front of my father and Uncle
Nevio by drawing on my repertoire—reading out imaginary menus ("Would you like the dead-toad lasagne
today, sir?") or improvising football-match commentaries. But as soon as they started to talk about politics, I
would run into the kitchen to complain.

"They're not listening to me!"

My godmother laughed, but my mother would look
at me with a vacant stare which was almost as frightening
as that of Polyphemus.

She had become completely dependent on Madamìn, the capable woman who helped with the housework. Madamìn was a widow with two children: she worked because she needed the money, but seeing her you would have thought she helped out of a disinterested generosity of spirit. Her smallest gestures had a noble dignity about them which gave her an air of authority. In her company my mother behaved like a little girl.

The day before New Year's Eve I burst into the kitchen with breaking news.

"Mommy, Mommy! Daddy said he'll take us to see the new James Bond film!"

"I'm not going without Madamìn."

I'd asked *her* to go with me. Wasn't that enough for her? Wasn't I enough for her?

"Go away, I hate you!" I exclaimed.

"I hate you."

I went and locked myself in my room, turning the key twice, and it took all my father's authority to get me to unlock it.

My mother clung to Madamìn for the entire duration of the film, *On Her Majesty's Secret Service*, the first James Bond movie without Sean Connery. He'd been replaced by some bargain-basement imitation.

Perhaps my mother too had been replaced? This

woman was no longer the mother I knew, and what happened that evening proved it. It was the last time I saw her.

———————

She'd called me to her bedside to apologize for her behavior over the Bond film. She'd hugged me in the old way, with her scented hair tumbling over my head.

I thought the mother I knew had come back, but all it took was a sudden bout of coughing and she started to behave like a feeble invalid again. In a plaintive tone of voice, she urged me once again to be good and kind towards everyone—to which my reaction was: "Yes, Mom, OK. Sleep well. Can I go now?"

"Sweet dreams, little one."

"I'm not little. I'll soon be taller than you."

"Of course you will be, taller and stronger. Promise me you will be?"

I couldn't put up with it anymore. I fled back into my room and, in protest, got straight into bed without brushing my teeth and fell immediately into a deep and dreamless sleep.

———————

Madamìn solved the mystery of the dressing gown left in my room. "Terrible Thing" had come to wake my mother during the night, but she'd asked him to be so kind as to wait while she came to tuck me up in bed . . . Afterwards, she'd forgotten to take her dressing gown and left it in my room. At this point the story always ended, as Madamìn started to cry.

I had no idea what my mother might have been feeling like when she was confronted with "Terrible Thing"— pretty bad, I guessed, even though mothers had always inexhaustible resources to draw on. But I knew it wasn't possible that only my mother had been able to persuade this thug to let her come and tuck me in.

It was clearly a tall story invented by someone with no imagination—in other words, Dad. He was trying to make me believe that my mother had gone on loving us right up to the moment she'd disappeared, whereas it was evident to me that if she'd run off with "Terrible Thing" it was because she'd had enough of us both. I could just about manage to understand how she might have grown tired of him—but of me? How could she have stopped loving me?

We suffer when we're not loved, but it's a greater pain when we're loved no longer. In one-way infatuations the objects of our love deny us their love in return. They take something away from us, which in fact they've only given

24

to us in our imaginations. But when a reciprocated feeling ceases to be reciprocated, a shared flow of energy is suddenly and brutally cut off. The person who has been abandoned feels like a sweet that tastes bad and is spat out. We've done something wrong—but what?

That was how I felt. I hadn't been able to make her stay with us. Perhaps she'd gone off to find a son who could do better drawings of her?

And yet I went on thinking she would come back, perhaps with the other son in tow. Never mind. I'd put up with any humiliation, just so long as she'd return.

five

In the meantime, while waiting, a spare mother would have come in useful. Unfortunately, as destiny would have it, none of the leading candidates for the role were still available.

Grandmother Emma, my father's mother from the Romagna, was one of those women who become the stuff of legends. The most scintillating story told about her was that as a girl she'd landed a wallop on the nose of a fellow Romagnolo—the future Duce—when he'd tried to take advantage of her on top of a haystack. The source of this piece of braggadocio was my socialist grandfather, but anyone who'd been on the receiving end of my grandmother's fists was inclined to believe the tale.

On another occasion—and this time there was

evidence—she'd forced a local builder who kept his work-men on starvation wages to pay them decently by bursting onto the building site near her home and brandishing a rolling pin still covered in flour over the man's head. She then threatened to use the same weapon on the workmen if they so much as thought of going off and spending the money in the local tavern rather than taking it home and handing it over forthwith to their wives.

At the age of thirty, she and my grandfather upped sticks and moved to Turin. During the day she worked as a concierge and in the evenings supplemented the family income in a pizzeria, baking *piadine al prosciutto* and *farinata*.

Her most prized possession was a tin box. On my grand-father's paydays, my grandmother would requisition his entire tram-driver wages by "de-wine right"—meaning he would otherwise have gone and spent them drinking with his chums—and stashed them away in the box together with her own earnings.

The accumulated hoard was divided up into three piles. One went to pay the bills, another was for daily ex-penses, but the last and most important one was set aside for my grandmother's own wishes. She would make a wish for something—a washing machine, a refrigerator, a sew-ing machine—and then started watching the pile grow week by week. Only over her dead body—which, like her personality, was on the large scale—would the rest of the family have dared to come near the tin box.

When the pile of money set aside for her dreams reached the set target, my grandmother would put on her Sunday best and take herself down to the shop, as proud as the Emperor of Cathay. Once the shop assistant suggested she buy something on a hire-purchase scheme: my grandmother fixed him with a stare as though he were a piece of pastry ready for her rolling pin. "Do you really think I'd go on paying for something I already own?"

That was my grandmother. I recall her sudden bouts of sulking, her hands like blades working the pasta dough, and her famous *cremigi* pudding, all yellow and black, which she would turn out onto an oval dish, letting me scrape off the hot chocolate sticking to the sides of the pan with a wooden spoon. My father got upset every time he saw me doing this, since he'd never been allowed to as a boy.

She had my grandfather so much under her thumb that when he died everyone thought she would barely notice he wasn't there. Instead, on account of one of those curious laws that keep together apparently unbalanced marriages, she herself died six months later, and in terrible pain—which my kindly mother did her best to alleviate right up to the last.

———

My grandmother had reacted to my parents' marriage by retreating into an epic sulk. She'd wanted my father to marry someone better off.

Dad was ruled by his mother, but the revolution brought about by love inspired him with enough energy to send my grandmother packing—and my grandfather, too.

"It's about time you wore the trousers in this house!" he'd shouted at him before slamming the door as he left.

For a long time relations between my father and my grandmother were strained. It was my mother who brought them together again when she agreed to live in her in-laws' house after the honeymoon.

The small community was founded on a single principle: power, sole and indivisible, resided with Grandma Emma.

Detailed rules dictated every aspect of daily life. Sunday was designated bath day, but filling the bathtub four times over was not allowed under the terms of my grandmother's charter. Therefore, the same water had to be used by the two members of each couple in order to reduce waste.

My mother reacted to all these acts of oppression with gestures of unconditional love. She didn't give expecting something in return—she just gave, without calculation, without reproach, without hope of reward. My father kept telling me this all my life, to underline just how different I was from her.

She was also gifted with an infectious laugh. My god-mother used to tell me how at my parents' wedding the priest had to halt proceedings because the bride couldn't stop laughing. When she managed to suppress her giggles, her eyes were still full of laughter—and so she even sent her gruff husband-to-be into fits of laughter as well. My parents took their eternal vows while laughing fit to burst.

My mother overcame Nonna Emma's prejudices by the sheer force of her character, and my arrival did the rest. They became firm friends. Walking between them, holding their hands, I felt safe.

Now there were only men left to walk next to me.

at least
David Copperfield
had an aunt

six

At least David Copperfield had an aunt. I would have to make do with my mother's four brothers.

The youngest of them shared her sensitivity of character and so ended up by injecting a feminine note into an atmosphere which was otherwise heavy with the smell of aftershave lotion. I took to calling him "My Uncle." I had a desperate need to bind the survivors to me.

One Saturday afternoon My Uncle took me to see my maternal grandmother, who was now in a rest home set among the rolling vineyards of the Langhe region. During the drive there I found out why I wouldn't be able to count on her.

Grandma Giulia's life had been filled with too many misfortunes and too many children. The youngest of these had been My Uncle. While she'd been pregnant with him she'd caught German measles and ever since had suffered from epileptic fits.

At the start of the Second World War her husband had died in her arms from a cold which a simple shot of penicillin would have cured, leaving her with a widow's pension and five hungry children. The eldest, my mother, had to shoulder the responsibility of feeding them on her own. At the age of sixteen she'd started work as a typist at the Fiat factory, while still looking after her mother and all her brothers.

I can testify to the fact that she continued to keep an eye on them. Our house saw an endless coming and going of awkward young men who would turn up to ask their big sister's advice on a variety of topics from their love lives and their jobs to what color of socks they should wear.

Mom would talk to them in the kitchen, the oracle's cave they would enter bearing the tribute of a box of marrons glacés. As the cook's assistant and official sheller of peas I had a privileged ringside seat at these incomprehensible conversations, punctuated with expressions such as "She's a nice girl" and "It's a secure job."

My Uncle was twelve years younger than my mother and thought of himself a bit like her son. He told me about the night when he'd ridden across the city on a clapped-out scooter to get to the maternity clinic where I had just seen the light of day. While the rest of the family bombarded the midwife with questions about me, he'd wanted to know above all how she was.

"The number of times she showed me your number twos!"

"What do you mean?" I blushed.

"You used to do your business in a potty shaped like a duck. Your mother used to carry it round the house, showing off the contents as if they were some kind of sculpture. She was crazy about you."

"So why has she gone away?"

It was obvious she'd liked me as long as I'd used the potty: when I'd started to sit on the toilet she'd stopped loving me.

"It wasn't her decision. It was fate . . ."

My Uncle lifted a hand from the steering wheel to put his sunglasses on so I wouldn't see he was crying.

––––––––

We arrived at the rest home and were taken through rooms packed with years. Would I ever see my mother's face all covered in wrinkles? Or would she always remain the young woman staring out from a photograph on one of the bookshelves at home? The pearl necklace and jersey cardigan she was wearing were doing their best to make her look old, but her girlish smile and bright-blue eyes, ready to be amazed at all they saw, gave the lie to that impression.

Nonna Giulia shuffled unsteadily in her slippers towards us. She clung to me more out of desperation than affection and dragged me into a room which looked out onto the garden.

"What have they done to my daughter?" she cried, before My Uncle had had a chance to extract me from her grip.

It had never occurred to me to think of my mother as someone's daughter.

I was amazed that no one had told my grandmother the truth about my mother going off with "Terrible Thing" after doing all her errands.

I was ready to tell her the whole story, leaving out only the puzzling fact of the dressing gown, but My Uncle dragged me off.

I would also have told her that the story wasn't over yet, and that she would reappear as unexpectedly as she had disappeared. After all, didn't all mothers have a special pass which allowed them to come and go as they liked?

Sitting in the passenger seat next to My Uncle, I made an effort to keep my eyes fixed on the road ahead. As the roadside advertisement hoardings sped past, I promised myself I would broach the subject as soon as the next one had gone by—but we reached home and I still hadn't plucked up the courage.

Certain questions frightened me. Or perhaps I was more frightened of the answers.

seven

When it came to my grandmothers, I'd had to admit total defeat, but the situation was not so dissimilar when it came to the other possible candidates for the role of deputy mother.

Madamìn already had two children of her own to look after and couldn't move in to take care of me.

My godmother was childless, but she and my father had fallen out. An icy antagonism formed between them, full of things unsaid. She and Uncle Nevio started coming round less and less, and then their visits stopped altogether.

My father shrugged this off by assuming a tough-guy stance: "You're really stuck if you have to rely on other people. We can count ourselves lucky: we don't need anyone's help."

Perhaps the thought occurred to me there might be a connection between the mysterious quarrel and whatever had happened to my mother—or perhaps it didn't and it's just hindsight painting a picture of me behaving like some underage detective in search of clues, whereas all I was was a little grief-struck boy who couldn't come to terms with the fact his mother had died.

———

My life had become void of female figures: the only women who remained were my primary school teacher and the mothers of my classmates.

My teacher had a large and capacious heart. She regarded the forty of us in her class like her adopted children. Far too many for an ordinary mother, but not for her: she saw into our souls, she knew when we needed to be scolded and when we deserved to be rewarded.

She'd been brought up in a socialist family and used to inveigh fervently against the Americans, who were at the time bogged down in the Vietnam War. I took note of her views and reported them back to my father, who adored the United States because they'd helped to drive the Nazis out of Italy. I was learning the elements of what would later become my job: taking note and reporting back—with a degree of emotional involvement, to be sure, but nevertheless aware there are always two sides to every story.

Dad never passed any comment on my observations. My parents never criticized my teacher. If I got a low mark in class it was because I'd deserved it, not because the teacher had it in for me. The earliest authority figures in my life had enough sense of their own authority not to want to undermine each other, and their presence gave me the reassuring sense I lived in an ordered universe.

This bright picture was blighted by my mother's disappearance: I was suddenly marked out as different. From being a little lord in a golden kingdom—gentle mother, stern father, but both guided by a sense of fairness—I found myself thrown out by the scruff of my neck into the dust.

I was the only one in my class not to be equipped with a loving mother. Despite all my teacher's careful efforts never to say the word "Mommy" in my presence, the discomforting sense of being an orphan combined with the worry that this was never going to go away, thus stirring up aggressive feelings towards others.

During my early school years, true to the star sign I'd been born under—Libra—I'd been a natural peacemaker, making strenuous efforts to pacify quarrelsome classmates.

Now, whenever I was provoked, I would give as good as I got, hitting back, blow for blow. What was the point of being well behaved if there was no longer anyone around to say "Good boy"?

————

The mothers of my classmates would give me pitying hugs, but cautiously, so as not to get dirty, as though I were some kind of bedraggled teddy bear which had fallen into a puddle. The way they hugged their own children was very different: it was the way my mother had always hugged me, with a kind of natural abandon.

It's hard to be without a mother in the land of mother-worship. It's true the Italians also enjoy being victims and the loss of a parent in early childhood, if displayed in the right way, can give you the status of a saint or a ticket for a free ride through life. However, when it comes to being a victim, you need to be cut out for the role.

I didn't want pity or special treatment: I just wanted to be loved. I wanted someone to be my number-one fan, but I knew that for all the other mothers there was always going to be someone else at the top of the list.

The despair I felt was carefully concealed under a show of pride, which took its inspiration from my father's stoical principle of the solitary hero sufficient unto himself.

I could never stand whingers. I never cried, even alone in my bed at night. I still believed that I'd wake up one morning and find my mother with her dressing gown on standing at the foot of my bed. I didn't want her to see my pillow wet with tears.

eight

Then Mita arrived. She was the babysitter who'd been given the task of bringing back some normality into my life.

I imagined she'd be a kind of Mary Poppins, showering me with kisses and chocolate cakes. My only concern was that she might turn out to be very beautiful and Dad would want to marry her.

So it was a relief when I first set eyes on her. She had as big a moustache as the school janitor. She bared her gums in a skeleton's grimace with a blast of bad breath which practically knocked me out.

"She's probably a nice person inside," My Uncle suggested.

He was wrong.

Mita had previously been in the service of a countess related to the Agnelli family and with a villa in the hills outside Turin. She regarded working for my father as a step down the social scale, and looking after me as a complete nuisance.

Still remembering the passionate hugs my mother used to give me, I tried to have the same physical contact with Mita. She turned out to be as rigid as wood, so I decided to try and win her over emotionally. But in that wasteland it proved impossible to leave any mark which could replace her nostalgic—and maliciously comparative—sense of the glorious years she had spent working for the now lost countess, the only time in her life when all had seemed like a fairy tale.

Mita was the first really dim person I had ever come across, and I found it impossible to adapt to her level of conversation. I wanted an audience who would listen enthusiastically to my monologues, but Mita was incapable of following even the simplest reasoning: our talks would leave me with a sense that I was either mad or had been completely misunderstood.

The only interest we had in common was the television. Mita could rightly regard herself as a real expert, with her thorough knowledge of the main textbooks in the field: the television guides *Sorrisi e Canzoni* and *Radiocorriere TV.*

For her, watching the telly was a kind of pagan ritual, where the various presenters and singers were the divinities. The heavens and the earth had been created in six days by the TV host Mike Bongiorno, who on the seventh had rested from his labors and handed over to Pippo Baudo's variety show. But the real watershed in the course of human history had been Gigliola Cinquetti's appearance at the Sanremo Music Festival. Many years had passed since that miracle had taken place, but Mita continued to bask in the longing for a lost paradise, back in the days when she would listen to Gigliola Cinquetti singing "Non ho l'età per amarti" as she ironed the countess's undergarments.

———

One Saturday evening in autumn, Dad went out to dinner with friends. It was the first time he had left me on my own in the evening, and the prospect filled me with twinges of anxiety.

Mita took over the sitting room and sat down in front of the television with *Sorrisi e Canzoni* open on her lap like a prayer book. *Canzonissima* was just about to start. It involved singers taking part in a competition in which the winners were chosen by the TV audience, who could send in their votes with their New Year's Day lottery tickets.

Mita was a decidedly floating voter, but her choices had a subtle consistency about them. She liked talented newcomers such as Mino Reitano or Massimo Ranieri. She told me the names of their girlfriends and other personal secrets until my attention was suddenly distracted by a mesmerizing vision which had just appeared on the TV screen: a woman's bare midriff with a belly button.

The woman who'd had the audacity to exhibit her belly button in public was called Raffaella Carrà. She came from Romagna, like my grandmother Emma, and she was blond, like my mother. She later reappeared in a miniskirt, kicking and twirling her legs, judiciously covered in dark stockings, in a variety of provocative poses.

I was still too young to perceive any glimmer of sensuality in what I was watching, but I was still stirred by the images. They succeeded in opening a breach in my hardened soul. When the dance had ended I plunged like a diver, holding my breath, into Mita's arms and kissed her hollow cheeks.

"You'll be my mommy won't you?" I pleaded, shamefully.

"I'm sorry, boy . . ."

That's what she said: boy. She didn't use my name.

"I'm sorry, boy . . . I can't love you. No one's ever loved me and . . . I don't know how to."

"I'll teach you."

It was true, I could just about remember how to.

"I can't . . . I'm sorry."

She brushed a hand over her eyes and hurried into the bathroom just as Massimo Ranieri came on stage.

That was the moment when I felt an iron curtain drop down within me. The illusion I could somehow regain the love I had lost, the imaginary world to which I'd clung for a whole year.

I now admitted to myself that my mother was gone forever and that no one ever again would love me, accept and protect me as she had done.

I buried my face in the sofa cushions and finally wept for what had happened to my mother. And to me.

nine

The candidates who might have replaced my mother had all fallen by the wayside, and I no longer had any hope of getting back the original. All that was left to me was Dad.

When a mother dies, you need men with feminine sensibilities to fill at least in part the abyss which is left. Men capable of being strict when necessary, but also sensitive. But my father was the epitome of masculinity. When he was growing up, his models had been two formidable men: Nonna Emma and Napoleon.

He had large hands and a fierce expression which intimidated me as much as it did strangers. An affectionate pat on the shoulder felt as though he'd hit me: he was as incapable of touching me gently as he was of making a decent cup of coffee. In the interval between Mom's death and Mita's arrival he was forced to take on a role for which he was entirely unsuited.

Each day, when school was over, the kindly mother of one of my classmates would give me a lift to the city council office where he worked. I'd sit tight at one of the corners of his desk waiting for the hour of release while doodling bunches of huge grapes on the backs of sheets of paper I fished out of the wastepaper basket. My mother had disappeared also from the drawings.

When my pen ran out, Dad would allow me to use one of the office pens, but as soon as the time came to go home he insisted I put it back where it came from.

"It doesn't belong to us. It belongs to the State."

I grew up thinking the State was a manufacturer of pens.

At two-thirty we sat down together at the kitchen table. It was the worst moment of the day, because everything in the room reminded me of my mother.

Dad would stand at the cooker and start to prepare lunch. His meals remained on my stomach and in my memory. I recall them with a kind of stupefied awe. They were so absurd they had a touch of genius about them. His specialty was tinned meat heated up.

A man with a feminine sensibility would have tried to find a babysitter capable of thawing my frozen heart. But my father regarded all such talk as so much hot air. The criteria he used when he chose Mita were the only ones he recognized: honesty and practicality.

I went back to eating tinned meat cold—cold like the rest of the house. In exchange I had to give up my bedroom for the new babysitter and resign myself to sharing my father's.

Mom's king-sized bed disappeared and was replaced by a pair of single beds covered by bedspreads sporting a pattern of black and brown lozenges.

The bedspreads were the least of my problems. My father snored like a bear who'd eaten a barrel of honey. The only solution was to get to sleep before the bear got into his den.

———

All our relationships are colored by a dominant tonality. The one with my father had been fixed forever when I was playing once as an infant on some meadow. I toddled resolutely towards the ball he had just thrown to me when I realized I was about to tread on a daisy, so bent down to pick it and give it to my mother.

She was touched; he thought I was unmanly. After all, in the biographies of Napoleon, which my father knew all by heart, was there an episode from the future hero's childhood when he'd decided to pick a bunch of daisies to give to his mother instead of expressing his will to power by bashing all and sundry round the head?

The incident dogged me for decades like a kind of self-fulfilling prophecy: "Besides, when he was little he once stopped to pick some daisies . . ."

Now that my mother was no longer there to cushion us both, the friction between our different temperaments lost its momentum and became instead a blind outburst of frustration from two victims incapable of understanding each other. It's true it cannot have been easy for him to live with a son whose physical appearance and to some extent personality reminded him continually of the wife he had lost, but I was too taken up in my own suffering to bother myself about his.

Talking about my mother was completely off-limits. Only once did I dare to ask him, in order to find out what the most awful thing which could happen might be in some hypothetical hierarchy of bad luck—whether it was worse to lose your wife or your mother prematurely?

It wasn't a philosophical enquiry, but a cry for help. Only a few months had gone by since I had discovered that women had belly buttons and my mother was never going to come back. I felt a desperate need for some emotional bond with my father.

We were in his car—a Fiat 1 24 Coupé, more appropriate for some slender Grand Prix driver than my father's massive bulk—on our way to see Giorgio and Ginetta for a birthday party.

He presented a very logical argument, which lasted the duration of three red traffic lights and was brought to a close with this solemn assertion, as he parked the car in reverse gear: we were both in a mess, but I was more in a mess than he was, since you can replace a wife, but you can't replace a mother.

We got out of the car and never mentioned the subject again.

ten

The only thing that connected us was our passion for Torino Football Club.

When I was five I thought the story of the Great Torino Team was a fairy tale. Dad would tell it to me to make me fall asleep, but luckily I never did.

I wanted to hear how it ended, and it always ended in the same way: after they'd won hundreds of matches and scored hundreds of goals, "those great lads"—he always referred to them in these terms, and it was the only time he ever had a lump in his throat—climbed on board an airplane bound for heaven and never came back.

Everything was clear, everything was perfect. Death didn't mean anything to me at the time. Two years later I'd find out about it, once again thanks to the

Toro team, who are good at teaching you some of life's severest lessons.

The day before a local derby against Juventus caught the flu. But no sooner had Mum gone out to get some medicine from the chemist's than I perked up.

After promoting a vase and the umbrella holder to the status of goalposts, I started to dance around in the hallway dribbling the rubber ball with my bare feet. I did everything by myself, even the radio commentary, pronouncing the name of my favorite player in a high-pitched voice.

"Gigi Meroni gets the ball, wriggles past one Juve player, then another, then another . . . What's he up to now? Unbelievable! He's coming back and dribbling past all of them again. Now he's only got the goalkeeper. He slots the ball through his legs, lobs it over his head, squeezes it under his arms . . . Meroni is through, in front of an open goal . . ."

The doorbell rang. It was Riccardo, the Juve supporter who lived on the second floor.

"Meroni's dead, Meroni's dead!" he chanted with that malicious glee you find sometimes in children.

"What do you mean?" I shouted at him, the ball still between my feet. "I'm Meroni!"

Out on my own, in front of an undefended goal.

"You're Meroni? You're crazy! Turn on the radio. He's been run over by a car."

No airplanes involved this time round.

I went to the derby with my father. Among the general mourning, Toro triumphed four–nil. The typical joys of a Toro supporter. The match was my baptism of fire, my official initiation into a sect of grumbling but indomitable fans who are always ready to face down the Fates.

———

Sundays followed an unchanging ritual. Over lunch Dad would list all the reasons why he wouldn't take me to the stadium that afternoon: all of them could be summed up by saying he was tired of spending time and money on a bunch of clumsy oafs who didn't deserve to be mentioned in the same breath as "those great lads."

He would peel an apple with surgical precision and then shut himself in the sitting room, where he would pretend to watch the telly while I started to dress: underpants and scarf in the team's garnet colors, and then whatever came to hand.

After mulling over the TV news, my father would get up and stand by the window, watching the fans queuing up at the stadium gates. Our apartment block was just across the street.

He watched them in silence for a while and then heaved a huge sigh, which sounded as if the sky had fallen in, then disappeared into the closet to put his shoes on. While he was doing this, he would shout out to me: "OK, we're going! But it's only for your sake!"

I'd been waiting on the landing already for ages, leaning on the flag My Uncle had given me, which was the color of blood and Barbera wine. We always arrived after the game had started, and each time I felt ashamed—just as when my father took me to school late. With my mother, I would never have been late.

Football fanaticism left her cold, but she'd had to learn to live with it.

One Sunday in spring, Dad had proposed to her a trip to some of the places near Lake Como which appear in Manzoni's classic novel *The Betrothed*. The poor woman agreed. She didn't know Torino had an away match scheduled that day near Lake Como . . .

They were sipping their cappuccinos in front of the castle which had belonged to Manzoni's archvillain—the Unnamed—when, feigning surprise, he pointed out a poster advertising the afternoon's match on display in the bar.

When they got to the stadium my mother demanded they buy seats rather than stand: she was already several months pregnant with another Torino *ultrà*.

I was born quite a few games later, but that was the first match of my life. It was raining and the result was a boring nil–nil. But it didn't matter—I was still safe in my warm box seat.

————

After Mom had joined Gigi Meroni and "those great lads," I was no longer sure of anything. I became taciturn—you could have fitted the monosyllabic interjections I came out with on any given Sunday into a matchbox.

Dad felt certain that I only cheered up when I watched Torino play, and so started to take me to all their away matches too. That really helped. I remember one game at Varese, when we were winning two–nil three minutes from the final whistle. Varese managed to scrape a draw and I spent the journey back throwing up.

Then the spring arrived and Torino started to climb the Serie A table little by little. One Sunday about Easter time we had a home match against Naples: if we won, we'd leapfrog Juventus and come out top. Just like "those great lads."

This time Dad and I turned up at the stadium an hour before the start. But that was not much use: we reached the ninetieth minute and it was still nil–nil. I looked at my father, I looked at the pitch, I looked at the crowd. Nothing doing anywhere. So I decided to call on God.

"Dear Lord, please let us score a goal. You've taken my mother, you owe me."

A few moments later the Toro's coach sent onto the field the smallest striker in the world. He was called Toschi and, like all good elves, he ran onto the pitch and hid among the blades of grass.

The goalkeeper was holding the ball to his chest: he passed it to the fullback, who passed it back to the goalkeeper, who returned it to the fullback, who was just about to kick it to the goalkeeper . . .

The elf had had enough. He came out from his hiding place, managed to get hold of the stray ball and stick it in the back of the net.

The crowd roared in excitement; no one noticed the eleven-year-old boy holding his hands in prayer and looking up at the sky.

"Thank you, God!" I yelled as I fell to my knees.

Yes, thanks a bunch. At the end of the season the referees disallowed two completely regular goals scored by Torino, and Juve beat us to the *scudetto* by a whisker.

That meant Riccardo could plaster the walls of the lift with pictures of his beloved "pajama boys" (my nickname for the Juve players, on account of their striped shirts).

My stomach was so churned up I ate only grissini for a week. I kept on asking myself what kind of a sadist God was in leaving me motherless while still a child and making me the supporter of the unluckiest football team on earth.

eleven

When I came to the end of primary school, the teacher who'd been my last bulwark disappeared too. I lost all my bearings and drifted without a direction. A new feeling seized hold of me and wouldn't let go—a demon clinging to my back and weighing me down, a soft spongy monster who fed on my doubts and fears: mistrust, rejection, abandonment.

I called him Belfagor, after the TV series *The Phantom of the Louvre* I'd watched as a boy. He'd been a near contender to Polyphemus in becoming my nightmare bogeyman.

Endless questions tormented me. Out of all the mothers there were in the world, how come mine had to die? My classmates were taken to school holding their mothers' hands, their mothers cooked them nice food to eat, when they were upset they could go and be comforted in their mothers' arms. Why couldn't I?

My little brain kept searching for an answer. If I'd been capable of lifting my eyes and looking around me, I would have seen the world was full of much greater problems: wars, epidemics, floods. But Belfagor was good at keeping my eyes down so I couldn't see beyond the narrow horizons of my own small existence.

Every so often my father would threaten to send me away to boarding school—for example when I left my dental braces on my plate in a restaurant. Or whenever I asked him to sack Mita and replace her with a human being.

I became an avid reader of stories about orphans. I kept *Nobody's Boy* and *Oliver Twist* under my pillow—but they weren't any comfort. I even envied the main characters. They were desperate, but so too were all the characters around them. So they never felt themselves to be different in the way I did when I ended up in a Catholic secondary school for boys full of kids from families much better off than mine.

———

I needed the presence of someone like my primary school teacher—and instead I got Father Skullhead.

His nickname came from the bone-chilling shape of his skull. The religious order to which he belonged had demonstrated the wisdom it had accumulated over the centuries by packing him off to Libya from where, following Qaddafi's purges of the Italian community, he escaped back to Italy in order to purge me. Whenever I rebelled against some tyrannical exercise of power—and everything seemed tyrannical to me—his hard, square knuckles would come down on the nape of my neck. Baring his gums like Mita, he would hiss, "I know you don't like me . . ."

It was true: I didn't like him. I was the antihero in a novel Dickens had never had the guts to write: the story of a little boy's life in which all the women around him are inexplicably removed so he is forced to grow up with a dried-up nanny and a priest who liked walloping boys round the head.

Dad had enrolled me in a private school because it was the only one he could find which would keep me incarcerated until the evening, so that he didn't have to bother himself about me while he was at work. It was an advantage not to have to see Mita in daylight, but there was a price to pay: the evening meal in the school canteen.

This is how I picture to myself the seventh circle of Hell: a gloomy rectangular hall smelling of unwashed feet, where a serving assistant not overly conversant with the rules of personal hygiene plonks potato croquettes down in the dishes with his bare hands; somewhere in the dark background outsized pans bubble away with a potion which has the magic powers of making hungry little boys willingly decide to fast.

The lids were taken off the pans and a new fragrance wafted through the room: the good old smell of unwashed feet was replaced by a filthy stink of rotting cheese. As the content of the pans was ladled into the tureens, Father Skullhead presided over the supreme rite by intoning the prayer with which we gave thanks to the Lord for our daily slops—risotto with chicken livers.

The first time I attempted to eat it I vomited it up, amazed to see there was no difference at all between the puddle of sick on the floor and the food which remained in the plate—a dark mush in the middle of which, floating about like the victims of a shipwreck, were the entrails of the animals that had been sacrificed in some terrifying ritual carried out by Father Skullhead in the inner sanctum of the kitchens.

For he it was who'd invented this exquisite dish: it was obvious from the zeal with which he patrolled the tables checking that we all had enough. Whenever he came across some delicate soul who'd just lost his appetite, down the knuckles would come.

I'd never called on my mother to help me out. It was as if I'd put her into deep freeze, in a dimension I couldn't reach. But the risotto with chicken livers forced me to make an exception.

"What should I do, Mommy? Give me a clue."

Strange: I'd always hated that expression, "Mommy."

A bright idea popped into my head when Father Skullhead was only two tables away. I needed to stay cool and move quickly. Holding my breath, I lifted the plate piled high with chicken livers and passed it over the heads of my neighbors to Rosolino, a boy capable of eating any-thing—he'd happily munch sweet wrappers and pen caps which had already been chewed by others.

Even Rosolino was disgusted by the chicken livers—but not enough to interrupt his continuous cycle of grazing. He greedily ladled up three huge spoonfuls into his mouth and handed the empty plate back to me just a second before old Skullhead bent over to give it, through his glasses, a beady-eyed examination.

Rosolino continued to empty my plate meal after meal, until on one occasion—one very dark day—he somehow dribbled back into the plate some black, half-masticated glob.

"Did your mother never teach you to wipe your plate clean?" Father Skullhead breathed over me.

He took a piece of bread, mopped the plate up with it and pushed it into my mouth.

I repelled the alien mouthful and spat it out: it landed on the cassock of the kindly provider. I was suspended for two days and Dad didn't speak to me until the summer break. We communicated by gestures.

Those were the years when students set fire to schools and attacked the police. I'd spat chicken-liver risotto over a priest, but no one regarded me as a hero.

twelve

Rosolino came from Sicily, and had arrived in Turin just at the right age to fall into Skullhead's clutches. If you believed his stories, his father made millions. But our classmates—fair-haired local boys—said he smelt. This, together with his southern accent, was enough to gain him admission to the school's "Rejects' Club."

Our shared experience of disgrace gave rise to a friendship which would come to an end each evening when we returned home on the schoolbus. We used to play at flipping Panini cards of our favorite football stars on the soft leather seats. If you could flip a card over so it landed picture-side up again you won the right to keep it.

Rosolino cheated, and so did I—but not so skilfully. Insults flew between us.

"Southern peasant!"

"Bastard!"

I didn't know what the word meant, and when I found out my friend had already moved to another city.

I'd told Rosolino—as I'd told everyone—that my mother never came to fetch me from school because her work required her to travel a lot. She sold Indian cosmetics.

Top marks for originality, wouldn't you agree? There must have been an occasion when an agent selling beauty products had called on Mom. I vaguely remembered a lady painting her nails pink. The Indian connection, on the other hand, was my very own dash of poetic license, inspired by recent events.

———

The Christmas holidays were like one long Sunday, made worse by the ghosts of the past. We never spoke about Mom, even when we visited the cemetery, where Dad preferred to focus on practical matters: buying artificial flowers because they lasted longer, wheeling the mobile steps to the appropriate vertical row of burial niches and climb up to the topmost one, where the photograph of the departed smiled out, making sure not to spill water from the vase (but what was the point of the water if the flowers were artificial?), then climbing back down again and wheeling the steps back to the exact spot from which he'd moved them.

We then stood there gazing upwards without speaking for a few minutes, before returning home to enjoy the rest of the holiday—my father in one room, me in another, and Mita in between watching television. At Christmas we turned down My Uncle's invitations—after all "we didn't need anyone's help"—both to dinner on Christmas Eve and lunch on Christmas Day. We didn't even need to find a separate set of excuses.

The football schedule took a break over the New Year, so we needed to find another way to while away the time. Dad was struck by the bright idea of going on a package holiday to India—from New Delhi to Benares, the holy city on the banks of the Ganges with its famous steps going down into the river, crowded with all the earth's outcasts. With our arrival, they could at last put up the "Fully Booked" sign.

There were lots of mothers in the holiday-tour group. Everywhere we went you'd hear their anxious instructions: don't touch this, don't go near that animal, stay clear of those beggars. Dad did his best to copy them, but he just didn't have their sharp eye or tenacity. The result was I always ended up in scrapes. I was probably the envy of the other boys on the tour.

I wish I could say I brought back some glimmers of spirituality from this pilgrimage of a widower and an orphan to the land of mysticism—but the only snapshots in my mental travel album consist of a series of humiliations, all of them profane.

Dad offering to buy a round of drinks for the waiters in the hotel—it was New Year's Eve—wherewith a party of high-caste Brahmins got up and left the room, giving us dirty looks on the way out.

Dad in a pink turban like some fake maharajah clambering up onto an elephant while I, dying from embarrassment, hid behind the column of a Hindu temple.

One of Dad's friends turning on a compatriot of Astérix who had managed to stab him in the hand with a fork in the daily scramble for the buffet and declaring in Franglais: *"Vous, français, très rude. Je suis proud to be italien!"*

Dad, again—I came across him in the hotel corridor planting noisy kisses on the cheeks of one of the women in the holiday group. She was blond and her short legs clothed in leopard tights poked out from her skirt like a pair of pythons.

At the time I pretended I hadn't seen anything, but as soon as we got home I wrote him a twenty-page letter—the gist of which was contained in the concluding sentence: "If you marry another Mommy, I'll leave home forever."

I didn't get a reply. But the python woman disappeared into the jungle, never to return.

real life had shown
itself to be a
bloodthirsty tyrant

thirteen

Real life had shown itself to be a bloodthirsty tyrant, so I asked for political asylum in the land of fantasy.

The sitting-room walls echoed with my radio football commentaries, improvised aloud while I flicked against their surface a blue headscarf with white spots that had belonged to my mother.

The flick produced a dry little noise, which led My Uncle to call the game *tick-tock*. He was the only person I'd initiated into the workings of this strange ritual enacted behind the closed doors of the sitting room.

As soon as I took hold of the miraculous scarf, my mind's eye would fill with pictures of a footballer who had my name and who managed to combine pure class and brute force. Each time he scored a goal, my double would wave his arms in the direction of an area of the public stands, where a woman recognizable only for her blond hair responded to the tribute by elegantly clapping her hands.

Whenever there was someone else at home—normally Mita, who was in most of the time—I took care not to raise my voice or I put a record on to cover the sound. But sometimes she would burst in unannounced and find me red in the face and holding my mother's headscarf in my hands.

"You're crazy. Just wait till I tell your father."

————

I used to sweat a lot. Day and night, summer and winter. Sweating was my way of crying.

Belfagor hated tears. Like all the monsters which attack our souls, he was convinced that everything he did was for my own good. He wasn't capable of giving me any love, but he could stop the world hurting me. All I needed to do was shut it out. He hated the truth: his mission in life was to show how I could escape from situations which might involve suffering. But even so he'd not quite given up on the idea of scraping together whatever odds and ends of affection were available by encouraging my self-destructive tendencies in order to attract the attention of others.

The most harmless of my neuroses—looking at my knees all the time—ended the day I started to wear long trousers. But in the meantime another more dangerous one had emerged.

———

As a little child I had welcomed the arrival of all kinds of germs with enthusiasm. My mother was an indulgent nurse. There was nothing better than having to spend weeks in bed with my face all covered in spots while she sat by my bedside and read me fairy tales or hummed songs. But then the nurse had abruptly handed in her resignation and I'd realized that even being unwell would no longer be the same thing.

So Belfagor filled me with the terror I might become ill. He'd enter my head unannounced and hiss his peremptory orders.

"Do such and such a thing or else you'll catch a bug."

The things I had to do were never the same. Stopping in the middle of crossing the road to take two steps backwards and one step diagonally. Pinch a passerby's bottom and then make a run for it. Aim a ball at the small painting of the Madonna in the headmaster's office.

They were usually actions which involved skills of precise physical coordination. Acts of pure vandalism were less frequent, and in any case were always followed by immediate repentance: once I spread glue all over a bus seat, but then I sat down on it myself.

The situation got worse one summer day at the end of an excursion into the countryside with Giorgio and Ginetta. We'd eaten our packed lunches and Dad stretched out on the grass for a nap. He was snoring. The nape of his neck gleamed about two feet from a tree trunk.

I was lolling in the grass at a safe distance, flicking a stone, when Belfagor spoke.

"You've got to throw the stone between the tree trunk and your father's neck. If you don't, you'll get ill—really really ill."

Too agitated to take aim with the proper consideration, I threw the stone: it hit my father right on the nape of his neck.

He reemerged from his snoozing limbo and lunged at me like some wounded animal.

I stumbled up a steep path with him in hot pursuit. With every step I took I was panting fit to burst.

"But, Dad, you don't understand. It was a test, and I've flunked it—and now I'm going to get ill!"

"You bet you will! Just wait till I catch you . . ."

————

But he didn't catch me, and the phobia of falling ill faded. It was replaced by a fear of burglars. Every evening I would go through the whole house inch by inch to see if they'd managed to get into the linen cupboard or were inside the washing machine. But perhaps I wasn't looking for thieves, but for what they'd stolen. Something that had been stolen from me.

Once, during my nightly inspection, the sight of a large box in my father's study awakened a memory from my earliest childhood. My godmother had come up to me looking perplexed.

"Where's your Mommy? I can't find her."

"Silly, she's in the kitchen!"

"Are you sure? Go and check."

I went through all the rooms calling for her, increasingly nervous and upset. I even looked to see if she was inside the cooker. I finally plucked up the courage to enter the holy of holies, strictly off-limits—my father's study—but all I'd found was a large box under his desk.

Then I started to cry, and my mother jumped out of the box and hugged me.

"Surprise, surprise!"

But I was furious. Children are serious-minded: they hate stupid jokes. They know that sooner or later they become real.

fourteen

After my missile attack on him, my father decided to send me to see a psychiatrist. He was actually just a general practitioner who'd studied psychology in his spare time. For my father to have sent me to a genuine psychiatrist would have meant admitting that I was genuinely mad.

Dr. Frassino's monologues were punctuated with long, exhausting silences—and I would come out of those slow-mo sessions more jittery than when I went in. I don't remember anything else about him except for one of his declarations:

"One's personality is formed during the first three years of life. Losing your mother at the age of nine doesn't lead to deep-seated psychological deficiencies, though it may reinforce certain underlying tendencies."

Let me translate: if the little one had lost his mom while still a toddler, he would go on throwing stones at his dad. But as he was a little older when she died, the worst thing that could happen is he'd tie one to his father's neck one day.

This was a time when everyone thought they had the right to pronounce on who I was. Father Skullhead had made us take a kind of crossword puzzle which he said was an aptitude test and declared that the secondary-school course best suited to the development of my talents was Accountancy. Even my father had to laugh.

I needed a factory producing good role models which could show me the way—and I found them in biographies. My passion for reading about the lives of others stems from the unconscious desire to discover how they managed to survive their first experience of grief.

I was obsessed with the idea that the loss of my mother when I was still a child would mark my existence forever and wanted to be reassured this was not the case. I remember reading that the Buddha and a Mafia godfather had both lost their mothers when they were children. But they'd taken different routes afterwards. Perhaps I too might come up with an acceptable compromise.

———

But I'd have been happy just to keep my feet on the ground. Instead I used to walk about on tiptoe like some kind of elf. The soles of my shoes were worn away only in front: my heels hovered in midair, quite uselessly.

I walked on the tips of my toes and kept looking down at them, since I was incapable of looking up, towards the sky.

I had good reasons not to. The sky frightened me—and so did the earth.

My Uncle came up with a piece of sensible advice: he told me to lift my chin while walking, as if I was trying to draw a line between my chin and my belly button.

I tried it out, making a real effort. I ended up walking straight into a lamppost.

In essence, the story of my life is the story of my attempts to keep my feet on the ground while looking up at the sky.

———

I may have gone around on tiptoe, but I could play football well enough with the other kids in the neighborhood. On summer afternoons I'd meet up with my acne-ridden peers from the area in the car park of an autoparts factory.

We divided up into teams of Toro and Juve fans; we tossed for the one Inter supporter. He was a few years older than the rest of us and took all the headers.

These were matches played until we dropped with exhaustion—and were almost invariably called off for reasons of "force majeure": a workman confiscated the ball because we dented his car; an old lady averse to noise threw buckets of icy water down on us from her balcony.

One evening, I was returning home after a memorable game—play suspended at 15–all because the ball had been impounded—when I was surrounded by a gang of thugs on motorbikes—lots of them—all of them much bigger than me.

"What you been doing to my little sister?" the gang leader inquired, grabbing hold of my sweaty T-shirt.

"Me?"

"Yes, you, shitface. What you done to her, eh?"

"You're mixing me up. I don't know your sister. I don't know you either."

Something long and black flashed out and turned into pain. I think they'd hit me with a chain.

I fell onto the pavement, and the bikers started a bizarre motocross, going round and round my body in ever decreasing circles.

"You want money? Take it!"

I threw them my wallet, but remembered too late it had nothing in it.

Their leader was not best pleased.

"My little sister was right. You're a real shitface."

"Shitface," "his little sister"—these were the only two concepts stuck in his head. Any effort to broaden the topics of our conversation seemed pointless.

His motorbike was poised to run over my legs when a man in a gray suit crossed the street. With a jerk of my torso I managed to lift myself up from the pavement and run towards him.

"Help, they're going to kill me! Take me home, please. I live near here."

The man in the gray suit took hold of my hand and we started to walk, with the bikers at our heels. Their leader had immediately sensed the man was a coward.

"Beat it, my friend, we need to give shitface here a little lesson. He treated my little sister bad."

"Don't listen to them!" I pleaded.

"What did you do to her exactly?"

Now the bikers had started spitting at him. He took a few more steps and then suddenly let go of my hand.

"I'm sorry, I've got a son too . . . I've got a son too . . ."

The sight of him escaping was so pitiful that my

torturers lost interest in hurting me. I scurried like a mouse into the safety of a baker's shop.

I soon forgot my attackers' faces. But the man in the gray suit often reappeared in my nightmares, together with an unanswered question: why did everyone abandon me—not only my mother, but even people I didn't know, when I most needed them?

————

The web of lies I wove to hide from the world what my life was lacking grew thicker. Until finally, a beam of light penetrated the rotten tangle.

On the morning of my thirteenth birthday, I woke up to find on my bedside table an LP of Barry White in wrapping paper.

"It's a gift from Sveva." my father told me.

"Who's Sveva?"

"A colleague of mine."

"She wears leopard tights?"

"Not that I'm aware of."

"And why has she given me an LP of Barry White? Never heard of him."

"Nor has she. She asked the shop assistant to recommend something."

"And who recommended Sveva to you?"

"Are you being serious or just joking?"

"It's a serious joke."

"I've never understood your weird sense of humor."

Dad liked telling shaggy dog stories. There was a Frenchman, a German and an Italian . . . He was good at telling them. At the seaside, during the summer holidays, everyone roared with laughter—Frenchmen, Germans and Italians. Everyone except me. I was always ready to rebel against his authority, but it still filled me with shame to see him put it aside and play the clown.

Sveva liked listening to my father's stories. She liked my father too. And she didn't dislike me either.

She came round to take a look at where we lived. The hostile glances she exchanged with Mita earned her a lot more brownie points, as far as I was concerned, than the Barry White LP.

Months later, in the summer, we—just the two of us— were going out to get an ice cream. When we got to the crossing, she took hold of my hand. I froze. I wasn't used to that kind of contact.

"Are you scared you might like me?" Sveva asked, giving me a kiss on the cheek.

A kiss. On my cheek.

"You kiss like a mother," I replied.

"I'll never be what your mother was. But I wish I'd known her, a lot."

"You'd have been friends. But I don't think she'd have liked to see you kissing Dad."

We laughed and laughed: we simply couldn't stop.

fifteen

Sveva had a grown-up son whom she'd brought up on her own after her husband had died. Not even for Sveva was I ever going to be at the top of her list.

Despite this setback, our alliance produced some notable results. We persuaded my father to pack Mita off to retirement and send me to the more academically challenging liceo classico—so much for old Skullhead's aptitude tests.

I remained in the same institution, but by promising to improve my marks and retelling the famous epic of the Chicken-Liver Risotto, it was agreed that I needn't stay on each day after classes were over and would therefore also be exempted from the culinary delights of the school canteen.

As if by magic, my afternoons and my bedroom were mine again. I divided up the time between poring over my Greek homework and letting off steam with games of *tick-tock.*

I'd introduced a variation into the game. I was no longer a football champion, but a rockstar. I'd put an album by Genesis—they and Pink Floyd competed for first place as my favorite band—on the record player, take hold of the magic scarf and—hey presto—I was transformed into Peter Gabriel.

In my head, I was on perpetual tour. Millions came to watch me—but as soon as I'd identified the one person among them all who interested me, I'd breathe softly into the microphone (the scarf I was clutching): "The next song is for you . . ."

Then across my mind's eye pictures of my double would flow, bathed in light as he strutted up and down the stage singing "The Carpet Crawlers." I didn't really understand the words, but Peter Gabriel's voice and the music were enough for me.

———

Meanwhile, thanks to the Toro, I also actually won the *scudetto.* It happened one Sunday afternoon in May. I was there—along with seventy thousand other people—as Graziani crossed the ball towards the boots of one of Cesena's defenders.

A normal person would never have tried a diving header anywhere near the boots of a Cesena defender. You would need to be a cross between an angel and a hero to do that. Luckily, my Pulici was that angel.

He made his Serie A debut the year my mother had decided to retire. He looked like an underfed Pinocchio and had large, fearful eyes. He could run so quickly he'd arrive ahead of the ball. But whenever he managed to kick it, he always ended up sending it sky-high or banging it against the advertisement hoardings.

My father said his feet needed realigning. Someone must have passed the tip on to the team's coach, since he immediately got hold of my angel-hero Pulici and made him train all day in front of a wall. In order to get his feet realigned.

Everyone forgot about him for a time, except for us children. The adults would go and watch the regular starters training, but we would huddle round the clearing where the thin Pinocchio played all by himself kicking the ball against a wall.

On one occasion the wall had had enough and sent the ball back right on Pulici's nose. My Pulici sank to his knees and buried his face in his hands, as if to hide the fact he was crying.

At this, I plucked up courage and shouted "Keep at it, Pulici!"

I don't think he heard me. Torino supporters shout softly—it's one of our peculiarities. But the fact was that from that day onwards his shots became more and more accurate, and his leg muscles more and more powerful. Until one Sunday the coach decided, without bothering to inform me, to select him again for the team for an away match in Cagliari.

I hadn't been able to go to Cagliari, as Dad was ill in bed with the flu, but when the radio commentator said that Pulici had taken the Toro into the lead I threw open the windows and yelled: "Keep at it, Pulici!"

I was so overjoyed I nearly fell out.

From then on he never stopped scoring. But all his feats were merely a long prelude to the Sunday afternoon when Graziani crossed the ball towards the boots of one of Cesena's defenders.

The angel swooped down to Earth as though he'd just spotted something he'd dropped a while ago. He buried his face in the defender's bootlaces and released the imprisoned ball, sending it on a journey which ended in the back of the net.

I opened my mouth to shout, but no sound emerged. My Pulici was running towards me with outstretched arms and closed fists. I saw the garnet-colored banners ripple like flying carpets and then lifted my gaze to the sky. They were all looking down: Gigi Meroni and "those great lads," up there, waving massive banners. Behind them, standing just slightly apart, there was a woman recognizable only by her blond hair who joined in the general rejoicing by elegantly clapping her hands.

———

I was stupefied with happiness. I'd been down to the depths too often: now I wanted to coast along on the surface, under the illusion that I was just like all the others.

Belfagor might have had something to say about it, but he'd grown less pressing of late. Perhaps he too was stupefied.

But the empty space in the family portrait remained a problem. Sveva lived with her son, and each evening Dad and I would go and eat with them. In the winter it was a kind of torture to fall asleep in front of the TV only to be woken up to go back home in the icy nighttime streets.

No one called on us. And certainly not my classmates. I didn't want them to find out that my home was smaller than theirs and with no sign of a mother. But there was always the risk that one day one of them might buzz at the intercom. I'd therefore taken down the photograph of my mother from the shelf and put it out of harm's way in the bottom drawer, underneath a pile of music magazines.

One evening in winter, when outside the snow was falling, my father called me into his study.

"What's happened to the photograph?"

I avoided his gaze.

"What photograph?"

"The one which matches that."

He pointed to the photograph of my mother enthroned behind the glass doors of the bookcase, standing like a sentinel in the midst of the serried ranks of biographies of Napoleon.

"I don't remember where I've put it."

"You're ashamed of your mother?"

I didn't say anything for some time, I'm not sure how long—but nothing compared to the seven years he'd never said anything to me. Then I said: "Tell me what happened when she died."

sixteen

Just before the summer, Mom found out she had cancer. She was operated on too late: the tumor had spread.

All those months when I grew convinced she no longer loved me, radiotherapy was wearing her body down, but she still made an effort to hide anything which might have alarmed me. She was always sad, but not on her own account. She was sad for us. She didn't want to leave us on our own.

On New Year's Eve, at dawn, my father woke up with a start and found she had gone into my room and was sitting on the bed. She was tucking in the blankets.

She'd reassured him: go back to bed, I'll stay here a little bit longer. The last image he had of Mom was of her head bent close to mine, while outside the window snow was falling.

Probably she'd suddenly felt unwell while she was in my room. A violent pain must have led her to take her dressing gown off. She crossed the corridor to reach the sofa in the sitting room, but she didn't manage to get there.

Dad had woken up again, almost immediately, as if he'd sensed something had happened, and he'd found her body huddled on the carpet.

He thought she might be still alive, but that illusion vanished when the ambulance arrived and the emergency doctor gave his verdict: my mother had suffered a massive heart attack.

She'd always had a weak heart, and the radiotherapy treatment, together with the spreading cancer, had weakened her resistance. But she'd fought to the very end in order not to leave us on our own.

"You should never be ashamed of a mother who did all that," my father said.

I went to look out of the window at the stadium across the road, covered in snow.

Perhaps she would have seen the snow falling. As the day of her death dawned, it was everywhere: in heaven as on earth.

I wondered if she liked snow. I didn't know. I knew nothing about her. This was the ideal prerequisite for turning her into a myth.

seventeen

Mom became my angel "without fear and without reproach," while the devil was the mother of one of my rich classmates. I would always see her at the end of the school day, draped with studied elegance against the boot of her jeep. Her hair was tinted blond, her lips painted an aggressive red, and her close-fitting jeans disappeared into long boots as black as her evil sunglasses.

I had a kind of nightmare. Over the Christmas holidays I would wake up at dawn and find that my room had been locked from the outside. I looked through the keyhole and managed to see a throne in the hallway and, sitting on it, the jeep blonde. She had attacked and killed my mother and invaded our house.

Two strangers were holding my father under the arms

and dragging him in front of her. The blond woman spoke. Her voice was icy.

"Give me the keys of the boy's bedroom, or I'll kill you too."

At this point Mita appeared, baring her gums and clutching a key.

"I've got a copy of the key, Countess!"

The blonde got down from the throne and marched towards my room.

I sneaked into the Submarine and through the spyhole of the sheet kept my eye on the door.

It opened. Across the threshold a pointed black boot appeared, and then . . . my mother with her kindly smile holding the teatime tray.

The same smile she had in the photograph I'd hidden away in the drawer.

———

Her portrait now took pride of place among the posters of Pulici and Peter Gabriel. I was sorry it couldn't speak to me: I would have asked her advice on a mysterious phenomenon which was beginning to intrigue me more than Genesis or even the Toro. Girls.

As a happy little boy, when life seemed like an endless

visit to the sweetshop and like some playboy I was always surrounded by women, the feminine held no mysteries for me.

My first love affair occurred one summer when we were staying at a hotel in the mountains. She had plaits and was called Cristina. She was seven years old and had an elderly lover—Antonello, aged ten.

One day Cristina came running up to me, squealing. Antonello had pushed her off the swing.

To punish him, I head-butted him in the stomach—he was tall and I couldn't reach any farther—and he repaid the kindness by beating me to a pulp with methodical precision. But it was more painful when I saw Cristina and Antonello together again on the swing. Now I think back on it, perhaps I wasn't such an expert on women then as I thought.

But Mom was there, and my wounded pride was soon forgotten. After a week of frenetic swinging, an irrevocable crisis occurred in Cristina and Antonello's relationship.

On the night when the first man landed on the moon, Cristina burst into the TV lounge, walked straight past the armchair where Antonello was sitting, as if he didn't exist, and came to speak to me.

"Let's go outside and look at the moon."

"But you can see the moon here!" Antonello's mother

objected, pointing to the gray grainy images flickering on the small screen.

Leaving aside the fact that Cristina had asked me and not her son, how could anyone prefer to watch television rather than the sky?

Mom seemed to read my thoughts.

"That's all right, just remember to put a pullover on."

And she gave me one of her famous hugs.

"Go and have nice dreams. Both of you have nice dreams. When you dream together dreams are even nicer."

Cristina and I stretched out on the hotel lawn looking up at the sky. The moon was three-quarters full and shone in the middle of a circle of stars, looking far closer here than it had done on the TV screen.

I pointed out to Cristina a mark darkening the wrinkled surface.

"Look, there's the spaceship!"

"That's not the spaceship. That's Arrosto," she replied, wincing in disgust at my ignorance. "Can you keep a secret?" she whispered. "Mommy told me that a long time ago an Italian went to the moon. He was called Arrosto, and he was riding on a hipposniff."

"Your mother doesn't know anything about it. My mother told me that Johnny Nose-snatcher lives on the moon."

"Johnny Nose-what?"

"If you tell a lie, he comes and cuts off your nose and takes it up there."

"Why?" the startled Cristina quavered, touching her nose to make sure it was still there in place.

"To eat it, obviously. He's eaten mine a dozen times."

I thought I'd managed to reassure her. But she suddenly screamed. A second mark had appeared on the moon's surface.

"Johnny is going to eat Arrosto's nose!" she exclaimed.

"I told you the story about the hipposniff was a lie."

"Shush!"

She grabbed hold of my hand, which made me feel peculiar.

From the half-open windows of the hotel you could hear the voices of the TV commentators quarreling about the exact moment of the landing.

"It's touched down! . . ." "No, it hasn't touched down yet!"

Cristina shook her head.

"Poor Arrosto! By the time the spacemen arrive, Johnny will have eaten his nose."

"Don't worry. It'll grow back."

You see, I've always had a weakness for happy endings.

eighteen

Since those days of the moon landings, I'd only been going backwards. I dragged my gloomy and clumsy self around a stage overcrowded with men. I was approaching the season of first love without knowing the slightest thing about women.

Dad's contribution was to send me back to Dr. Frassino, the pseudo-psychiatrist. He asked me to drop my pants and checked the size of my penis to make sure my childhood trauma hadn't shrunk it.

"Everything in order," he said, "you'll get a lot of joy from it." Here endeth the lesson of sex education. As for my sentimental education, Father Nico's maxims took care of that: "When a woman looks at a horse, she sees only a horse. But men perceive the horseness of a horse."

Father Nico taught Greek, Latin, religion—in short, most things. He regarded women as decorative objects, like the swirls of icing sugar on a cake. He used to say that before we got married we should make our fiancées write an essay. But it wasn't clear who would mark it. Father Nico himself, probably.

Had he been born in the Middle Ages, he would have been a Knight Templar—but he was happy enough being the Catholic version of the Übermensch. He slept three hours a night and read continuously, even while eating and walking, busily cultivating implacable obsessions.

"I am all for freedom of choice. If you're right wing, then vote for a right-wing Christian Democrat; if you're left wing, then vote for a left-wing Christian Democrat. The important thing is to vote for a Christian Democrat: against divorce and against abortion."

The year we took our school-leaving exams, on the eve of our first electoral vote, we organized a mock election in the classroom and wrote the results up on the blackboard.

When Father Nico saw that almost everyone had voted for the RP, he gave us an impassioned speech. As far as economic matters were concerned, he was in full agreement with the Republican Party—yet, it was still a secular movement, and it was his duty to warn us of the possible risk that it might take the wrong path in ethical matters. No one had the heart to tell him the initials stood for the fervidly anticlerical Radical Party, which in Father Nico's view was an unassailable proof of the Devil's existence.

————

In order not to take time away from the lessons, he subjected us to oral tests between seven and eight in the morning. I loved Greek—the dance of the gods—but hated the study of Latin—a march of soldiers. I developed a genuine passion for Homer, even though it was he who'd inflicted Polyphemus on me as a little boy, whereas I considered Virgil to be an overrated court sycophant.

One winter morning at seven o'clock Father Nico asked me about Book VIII of the *Aeneid*, which I had proudly disdained even to open. The pages were still uncut, and I had to tear them apart using my fingers as a paperknife.

"Translate from line 26 onwards. *Nox erat et terras animalia fessa per omnis.*"

"*Nox erat* . . . It was night . . ."

"Go on." And he spat out a piece of one of his fingernails: he had the habit of biting his nails and then distributing them freely in the vicinity.

"*It was night* . . . Does that even scan?"

"What did Horace say? *Quandoque bonus dormitat Homerus.* Every now and then even Homer nods."

"Please leave Homer out of it, Father. He's in another class. Virgil doesn't just nod, he snores and splutters . . . An illiterate gladiator could have written 'It was night.' Or the Met Office."

"Go on with the translation!"

"I've never understood why Dante in the *Divine Comedy* chose Virgil as his guide instead of Homer. Yes, I know, Homer was blind. But even so he could have had Plato, Aeschylus, Sophocles, Euripides . . ."

"A bold but interesting theory. I'll give you half a mark extra, two and a half instead of two."

"Just because I didn't like a line of Virgil's?"

"No. Because you didn't even make an effort to read the following lines. And because you deliberately started an argument, thinking I'd forget to ask you about them."

I assumed my classic madman's posture (closed fists, staring eyes, jutting lips) and jumped down from the teacher's platform, pursued by one of Father Nico's flying fingernails.

"Come back here!" he shouted.

And, in a lower voice, "I know life was harsh on you when you were little."

"Really? And who told you that?"

It certainly hadn't been me, since I was still sticking to the story about the agent for the Indian cosmetics firm.

"You think you can pay life back by refusing to grow up. But you only succeed in hurting yourself. You're always ready to start an argument, always on the attack."

"If once in a while someone would bother to give me—rather than Virgil—a bit of support . . ."

"Yes, that's right, you've got your excuses all ready! The poor victim surrounded by a hostile world."

"It's not an excuse. If I . . ."

"Only failures use the word 'if'! You achieve greatness in life *in spite of.*"

But he still increased my marks: he gave me a 3–.

———

Amid the rustle of cassocks, the only form of female life was the daughter of a colleague of my father's who gave me drawing lessons (I'd not progressed much beyond the depictions of giant bunches of grapes). She had a vast wardrobe of miniskirts and black tights. I was always bending down pretending to tie up my shoelaces in order to get a glimpse of her legs under the desk. She disappeared the day she found out I was wearing loafers.

I used to dream about an ideal sister wearing a miniskirt and black tights who would bring some relief to my solitude. Perhaps she wasn't a sister: more a girlfriend, or a mother. All three of them combined. I never understood why some of my classmates and their girlfriends were continually quarreling. Instead of rowing with them, they could have lent them to me.

There wasn't even the possibility of sharing a desk with some girl I could write poems to or whose breasts I could take sly glimpses of. We had to make do with what was available—in other words the girls' school at the corner of the block, a pack of demure young maidens who wanted to but felt they really shouldn't. "Don't do that, cos you know I like it," they would moan as some of the older boys gave them a hug. All they said to me was, "You're really cute"—a sure sign the road ahead was closed.

As a teenager, I divided girls up into two categories: unreachable virgin madonnas and disposable Red Cross nurses. You don't seduce virgin madonnas: you worship them. I worshipped them and at the same time was tormented by their indifference. Yet, as soon as they showed some interest in me, they lost all their appeal.

In order to avoid the possibility of being dumped, I only allowed myself to go out with girls I thought I could control in some way. Showing a lack of commitment was my speciality.

"Do you love me?" they would ask. I would count to 11 (Pulici's shirt number) and then come out with a series of inconclusive answers: a) I don't know; b) I'm afraid; c) I'm afraid I don't know.

Thinking back, I must have been a real idiot—and of the worst kind, an idiot who doesn't even know he's an idiot.

And yet, was I really like that? Or is hindsight massaging my memories in order to paint a flattering self-portrait? Being an idiot—and not knowing it!—is less of a humiliation than being a coward.

When I went to the wedding of Sveva's son, I realized that not all orphans are the same. Those, like him, who lose their fathers when they're children feel at ease among women. They never fall completely in love, since no girl they meet could ever live up to their supermoms, but this impediment just becomes another part of their charm.

Whereas losing your mother makes you less appealing. Not so much a solitary titan as a bedraggled chick.

Come to think of it, I've never mixed with other men who lost their mothers in childhood. Meeting other members of the club would only have undermined my belief I was unique.

In order to soften the impact of the real world, Belfagor had dulled all my senses. Nothing really enthused me, not even transgression. I didn't get drunk, I didn't take drugs, I didn't smoke joints (an occasional cigarette on an empty stomach was the limit of my daring). I didn't enjoy extreme sports or all-night parties: I've seen the sun rise more often waking up early than coming home late. I wasn't left wing or right wing: I supported the Liberals—which when you're eighteen is like preferring lemonade to tequila.

Political utopias made me anxious—just as emotions, dreams and suchlike did. And just as my mother did. I stopped adoring her and became indifferent. I no longer hid her photograph, but simply forgot it was there.

My spirit coasted along close to the ground. I didn't believe in anything, except perhaps in a few songs. Studying materialist philosophy and spending too much time in the company of priests had turned me into a mocking atheist. God was man's invention, and death was the end of everything.

When during the Ash Wednesday service the priest smeared my forehead, I laughed in his face. I knew all too well I'd end up as dust again, just as I knew nothing remained of my mother other than dust.

in every young man's
heart there's a
need to escape

nineteen

In every young man's heart there's a need to escape, and the best way ever discovered to escape from yourself is to fall for someone who isn't right for you.

At university I met Alessia—extremely tall, beautiful and vain—my "Miss First Times."

It was the first time I accepted the risk of someone turning me down (on the contrary she said yes before I'd even finished asking)—the first time I succeeded in unclasping a girl's bra with a single, elegant flick of the wrist—the first time I made love. As so often happens, it wasn't a particularly memorable experience: Alessia seemed to be more concerned about not spoiling her makeup, and I felt like a thief who finally breaks open the safe and finds it empty.

She became my girlfriend while continuing to surround herself with a court of silent admirers, whom she kept in a state of permanent uncertainty, playing with their infatuation just for the pleasure of exercising her charm over them. She was one of those emotionally dangerous people who pride themselves on their egotism thinking it shows they're sensitive.

I was the last person capable of becoming her moral tutor. "Have nice dreams," my mother had told me: here I was, trampling all over them.

In the hope of becoming a journalist, I wanted to study literature or political science at university, but my father continued to nurture Napoleonic aspirations for me: he saw me graduating in economics and then becoming a leader of industry.

I didn't fight for my dream, for the simple reason I was deaf to it. Our dreams are rooted in our deepest selves, and my deepest self was out of order.

So my father and I found a compromise solution which satisfied neither of us and was therefore entirely acceptable: I should study law.

"If you end up a complete failure in everything else, at least you'll turn out to be a lawyer like your mother always dreamed you would be," was the way my father, with his characteristic pragmatism, summed up the situation.

But I alone was responsible for the mistake. I'd chosen the wrong university course and the wrong girlfriend because I was too scared to listen to my dreams. It was obvious I was setting myself up to fail.

————

Alessia dumped me during a telephone conversation, moments after telling me she still loved me. All my defenses collapsed and Belfagor moved back in.

After some pathetic attempts to try to win her back, I stopped going to classes, closed the shutters and barricaded myself in my bedroom.

Is the ability to move on the recipe for a successful love life? I don't know. But if you lose out you stay exactly where you are. I sat for hours on end at my desk: my only comfort was listening to The Police and smoking Camel Lights ("Lights" sums up all my cowardice).

I'd studied a bit of psychoanalysis for the course in criminal anthropology and, armed with this smattering, I drew up a vast dossier on myself in which I stated various presumed truths in a dry unemotional tone and using the third person.

In the chapter entitled "Diagnosis" I wrote: "Since the trauma caused by his mother's death has alienated the patient's real self, everything he does, thinks and says does not originate from his own self but rather from a dysfunctional personality which has developed over the years and might be said to have taken over his life."

But how could the patient recover his real self? The chapter entitled "Prognosis" dealt with this question. It had as many "shoulds" and "musts" in it as any politician's hustings speech.

"We must deactivate the intellect and the senses, both of which have been unavoidably compromised. The instinct, as the only structural component of personality unaffected by the trauma, should be freed."

These were not straightforward problems. What could put me in touch with that "structural component" if not my—now completely superannuated—intellect and senses? But, even more important, who was to say that this entire dossier was not the product of the dysfunctional personality who had usurped my life rather than of my authentic self?

In this way my self-analysis got so tangled up in itself that it took weeks to find a way of extricating it. Then, one Sunday morning, as I was opening the windows to air the smoke-filled room, something suddenly dawned on me: if I wanted to recover my real self, I needed to open the windows there too and let the fresh air in.

It had nothing to do with setting off in a car or on a train: it was an interior journey I had to undertake. I would erase my past life, setting the hands of the clock back to the first morning I'd woken up to find I was without a mother. I fixed the precise time my new life would begin: 11:11 on the following day. But, when the time came, I happened to be sitting on the toilet, hardly the best place for an initiation ceremony.

So Belfagor agreed to give my real self another twenty-four hours, which turned into forty-eight—and then seventy-two. I'd got stuck again.

After further bouts of reclusiveness and raving, one evening I exultantly burst open the door of my bedroom to tell Sveva, the only person with whom I'd maintained at least the appearance of human contact, that I'd finally found the solution. In order to find my real self I needed to readjust the balance which had been destroyed when my mother died by bringing her back to life as well, through imagination.

If I could have done, I would have drawn her—this time without a bunch of grapes in her hand. All I did, instead, was try and bring her ID details up to date.

She'd have been fifty-six years old—still looking young for her years, although (I liked to think) perhaps a tad overweight: she'd always had a sweet tooth.

What would her voice be like when she spoke to me? I no longer remembered how it sounded. Her blond hair—I'd lost the sensation of its fragrance—what color would it be now? And her clothes? Would the wardrobe in which I used to play hide-and-seek as a child still be full of the same two-piece suits?

I circled round and round my mental cage. It was a prelude to madness.

———

One day I ventured out onto the landing and saw Palmira—now on her own after Tiglio had died—surrounded by shopping bags. She took a look at the dark rings under my eyes, the scrappy beard and the thinning hair at the back of my neck. Despite her understandable hesitation, she stroked my cheek.

"You're no longer the laddie I remember. You've got cold. If you'd had some warmth round you when you were growing up, if your poor mother had been alive . . ."

"Only failures use the word 'if'! You achieve greatness in life *in spite of.*"

I'd defended myself by parroting Father Nico's *How to Become an Übermensch,* but I knew my self was dead and done for. Even Palmira said so.

Her words kept echoing in my head. I could feel them going down my stomach, floating around in some acidic puddle and then trying to climb back to my heart.

It wasn't easy to overcome the obstacles Belfagor had put in the way. But a feeble voice did get through.

"*If* you'd grown up with your mother, you'd be less scared now of falling. But you'd also feel less of a need to fly. *In spite of* the fact she's no longer with you, it's time to start using your wings."

twenty

I suddenly didn't care anymore about becoming my "real self." Just becoming someone would be enough. Better still if that someone were someone else.

I had to do something, though. The monsters which prey on our hearts feed on our inertia. They don't grow because we are defeated, but because we give up.

I emerged from my prison cell and went back to university. I got top marks on my Criminal Procedure exam. I needed to take six more courses before I could graduate. I asked old friends who'd started their studies with me to give me a hand. But they were all working on their theses and didn't have time to turn back and help me catch up.

Once again I shut myself in my room. I drew up study schedules that I updated on an hourly basis. But working on my own on subjects which didn't really interest me just served to remind me how much my present life had become the result of all the defensive choices I had made in the past.

I needed to escape, and asked My Uncle if he could give me a job in his firm. It was exactly what he wanted, but not now—first I had to get my degree. He belonged to the last generation who had a real respect for education. At Christmas I used to give him abstruse philosophy books, which he would devour with an immense if disorderly hunger for knowledge.

I sought distraction in laddish Saturday-night pursuits, but the chosen companions weren't up—or down—to the task. I used to go about with a group of engineering students, all solid prosaic young men who dismissed my inner torments as mere whims and introduced me to nice but utterly forgettable girls.

They didn't even know I didn't have a mother. Or at least they didn't know it from me. I never broached the topic, and the fact that Sveva was around—after her son had got married she'd moved in with us—dispensed me from the need for further explanations.

Young men often find a cure for their existential malaise in politics or theater. But I didn't have the energy to cultivate creative talents. As for ideologies, I regarded them in the same way as I did love: to me, they were utopias that were totally incompatible with the egotism of human beings, especially my own.

Sveva suggested I go to the gym in an attempt to work off the toxins I'd accumulated, but when a pair of instructors with bronze-statue physiques—whom I nicknamed the Pillocks of Hercules—proposed a course of steroids so I too could have a body like theirs, I never set foot inside the place again.

Psychoanalysis remained an option, but sessions on the analyst's couch would have meant overcoming my embarrassment and asking for money from my father, who considered digging around in one's brain a loser's way of wasting time.

————

There are a lot of "buts" in the last few sentences, I realize. At the time it was my pet word. I felt as though a wall of incompatibility constantly loomed over me—as if anything I undertook, all my short-lived enthusiasms, would sooner or later disintegrate against it.

The law books on my desk I was supposed to be studying gradually made way for self-help manuals.

Taking Your Life in Your Own Hands.

The Art of Winning Friends and Influencing People.

Overcoming Neurosis.

How to Solve Your Problems and Start a New Life.

I used to highlight the important sentences, but I'd highlight more and more with each reading, until the pages were completely colored in orange.

I learned the following by heart:

- Björn Borg's opening speech at a tennis course run by the Swedish Tennis Association: "If you lack self-confidence, you're going to lose control of your movements";

- Kipling's "If": "If you can dream—and not make dreams your master / If you can think—and not make thoughts your aim";

- the anonymous poem "Found in Old St. Paul's Church in Baltimore," which touched upon the same themes but with less literary style: "Do not be cynical about love, for in the face of all aridity and disenchantment, it is perennial as the grass." As if on cue, the flower bed outside my apartment block had just been concreted over.

––––––––

I even managed to turn *The Great Gatsby* into a self-help manual, identifying with the likeable crooked hero of the novel tangled up with an unsuitable woman. Ever since childhood, Gatsby had been trying to improve himself, filling his pockets with reminders: "No more smoking or chewing; read one improving book or magazine per week."

I started to fill my own pockets too: "Do eleven sessions of press-ups a day and learn Spanish."

The two volumes for Commercial Law on my desk remained unopened, but for a month I studied Spanish and did a lot of press-ups.

Then suddenly, without warning, I packed that in, like a stage set being dismantled, and abruptly put up another: "Listen to the whole of Mozart and read the complete works of Jung. After eleven weeks, give Alessia a call."

———

But not even two weeks had gone by when Sveva burst into my room, shutting the volume of Jung and turning Mozart off.

"Do you think I can't see how you're leading your father on? You're not following your courses, you do the exams only when you feel like it—you may even have stopped taking them. Someone with your abilities—you should be ashamed of yourself."

She burst into tears.

"I don't think I deserve your tears," I replied sententiously, but secretly pleased.

"Your father and I are splitting up. He says he wants his freedom back. In a few years he'll be as old as your grandfather was when he died, and he wants to make the most of the time left to him."

"Dad's scared of dying, and I'm scared of living. Perhaps we could swap."

"He says we should leave him in peace and he'd be all right."

"And what do you want me to do about it?"

"Study! He says he's unhappy because you won't get on and take your degree. You're a disappointment to him: he's lost his faith in the future because of you."

"We're quits then. Can't you see he's just using me as an alibi to get his own way?"

"If I were your mother, I'd give you a good smack. I just hope that wherever she is now she can't see the state you've got yourself into!"

"Don't even mention my mom, OK? Get out! Or I'll go instead. That way you can get at each other's throats without putting me in the middle."

That was it. I'd managed to break the last thread of human kindness in my life.

Belfagor must have been really proud of my progress.

I thought I heard him murmuring his usual instructions in my head:

"You'll always be different from the others; no one will ever really love you."

———

I remembered it was summertime. I fetched the Canadian tent from the cellar and went off to join my engineering chums on a campsite on the Adriatic. But if you're sick in your soul, you can't solve your problems just by changing hospital. I hated my friends, I hated the camping site, I hated the Adriatic and every other sea in the world. I hated myself.

One morning I woke up with an excruciating pain at the back of my jaw. It was my wisdom teeth. I was twenty-five and they'd decided to come out.

The instinct for survival took over. I was capable of throwing my life to the dogs, but I wasn't going to be treated by a dentist I didn't know.

I took the first train back home. I closed my eyes to try and deaden the pain as a hazy memory from the long-distant past resurfaced, bringing the image of a pair of black-framed glasses bent down over my face.

I try to escape their investigative stare, but I can't,

because I've got a drill stuck in my mouth. The buzzing of the metal beast finally dies down, and I turn my head to see if I'm still alive—and the black-rimmed glasses become a complete face which is talking to my mother and telling her my tooth needs to be removed.

I scream, and the dentist shows signs of impatience. Then he leaves the surgery and goes into the room next door to do something or other with a filling.

"Try to calm the boy down before I get back."

"I'll calm him down, Doctor, don't worry," my mother replies.

She comes up to the chair, removes the bib round my neck and slips her hand into mine.

"Quickly, let's go!"

We're outside in a moment, but a drill-like voice echoes in the stairwell.

"Where are you going, signora?"

"I've just remembered I need to collect something from the dry cleaners."

"The dry cleaner won't close for three hours."

"The traffic is really bad today."

We run into the street and give each other a hug. Mom tells me about when as a girl her wisdom teeth had grown and how she'd come up with all the excuses under the sun to avoid going to the dentist to have them taken out.

"What happened then?"

"And then I had them taken out. After a while. We'll have your tooth taken out as well, my poppet. Just as soon as we're both a bit less scared . . ."

twenty-one

My wisdom teeth turned out to be so wise that I had to spend the mid-August bank holiday in Turin.

During a game of mixed doubles (two tennis players and two—one was me—who could barely hit the ball) I got to know Alberto, whose summer plans had also gone wrong and who worked for the *Corriere dello Sport*. One evening I accompanied him to a Toro match, wrote my impressions of the game on a crumpled piece of paper and gave it to him.

A few weeks later he left to do his military service, and his boss asked me to come and take his place. He was called Orso, and he was the first journalist I had come across. After my conversation with him, I thought he would also be the last.

He was waiting for me in the entrance hall and kept me standing like some petitioner. "Alberto gave me a zany piece to read and told me you'd written it," he began. "I haven't worked out if you're mad or you've just had a difficult childhood. The two possibilities are not mutually exclusive, of course. But I'm inclined to think you're mad. Which means we'll get on fine together. Your main job is to bring me my coffee from the bar without spilling half of it on the stairs. I must warn you from the outset: a permanent job is out of the question. But even in the most unlikely event you might one day succeed in fulfilling your nightmare of becoming a journalist, please accept right away my condolences, because it's a shit job. So, are you on?"

I said yes and started to type out brief delirious articles on local sports I'd never heard of such as *balon* and *tambass* for a thousand lire a piece: enough to buy a coffee and a bun.

I was finally somebody.

I'd achieved quite unexpectedly my dream of becoming a writer just when I thought I had given up wanting to become one. If you've got a dream and it's your dream, the thing which you've come into the world to do, you can spend your entire life trying to hide the fact under a cloud of skepticism, but it will never let go its hold on you.

It'll go on sending out desperate signals—like boredom and lack of enthusiasm—in the hope that sooner or later you'll rebel.

I reached a truce with Belfagor. I would stop probing into my wounded soul, while he agreed not to undermine the dream I'd just attained by inducing a collapse of self-confidence.

I didn't carry many coffees up the stairs, but I wrote a lot of stories, which gradually became articles. At first only my initials appeared beneath them, but afterwards they were well and truly signed with my name and surname.

So that I might be able to pay for an extra bun or two in the morning, my boss, Orso, managed to get me a job as a contributor to the sports pages of *Il Giorno* in Milan. Life is a master at irony: it turned out they only wanted pieces on Juventus.

In the meantime, Dad was splitting up with Sveva. It was a long-drawn-out process, with lots of rows and reconciliations. She continued to ask me for help, but I acted as if I didn't know anything about it. Belfagor had taught me how to behave in these cases: steering clear of any situations in which getting to the truth of the matter was bound to lead to suffering.

My father too seemed to have been infected with the same disease I had, and in order to distract himself from his own worries started to take an interest in my transformations. He was like a fencing master who knew exactly where his opponent's weak points were. In my company he would make scornful remarks on the futility of journalism as a profession, but he would read out my articles to his colleagues as if a new Hemingway had come on the scene.

It was a battle of nerves between us—and, strange to say, I managed to deal with it. In this I was helped by the thought that I had found a job and possibly a career without having to call on his support. Once, however, I made the mistake of asking him if Mom would have been proud of my choice of profession.

"Poor woman," he replied. "She must be turning in her grave. She wanted you to have a proper job, a secure one. You'll never get a permanent contract from a newspaper . . ."

———

The following mid-August bank holiday, all dental problems a thing of the past, I was basking in the heat of a telephone box somewhere in the middle of Sardinia.

"This is the editor of *Il Giorno* speaking," the voice at the other end of the line was saying. "I really like your articles on Juventus. I'm a Juve fan and I've read all of them. I wanted to ask you if you'd consider joining our team."

"Sure, I'd love to. But I'd need to win the lottery first if I am to live in Milan on a freelancer's pay."

"I think you've won it—we'd like to offer you a job. But don't get too excited: we've just lost our leading sports writer and can only afford to replace him with someone young who won't cost too much. So, what do you think?"

"What do I think? If it's OK? Whey-hey!"

I hung up and made eyes at the red-haired girl who was smiling at me on the other side of the glass door. Then I half-closed them: I needed to make an internal phone call.

"I've got a permanent job after just a year of training! And I'm in love, at last! Mom, if I'm ever going to join you, let it be now. There won't be a better moment to die."

So it had happened. Writing had emboldened me to such a degree that I could break the agreement with Belfagor unilaterally.

I'd fallen head over heels for the girl. Bonfires and guitars on the beach, lounging by the sea and inside my sleeping bag. All of us, once in our lives, have the right to believe those summer pop songs are written for us and us alone.

Like my paternal grandmother she was called Emma. She shared the same stubbornness of character too. All the boys in the group wanted to sleep with her, but she was considered off-limits, since her boyfriend was a Hulk lookalike. He'd been her dream man—and still was, even though they'd broken up just before the summer holidays and he was now showing off his muscles round the world without her.

I'd succeeded in seducing Emma—much to everyone's surprise (including, to some degree, my own)—by implementing an infallible strategy: listening to her. Women are not won over with our vocal cords but with our ears: it's a waste of time trying to impress them with memorable remarks when all they want is for us to pay some attention to what they're thinking.

I emerged at dawn from the sleeping bag feeling I was on cloud nine and ready to plan the next hundred years of my life with her.

She was as drunk with amazement as I was, but much more down to earth as well: she started to pick up the discarded beer cans littered along the beach, while I worked off my pent-up excitement by drawing the outline of her face in the sand, with my big toe.

A friend of hers asked me if I was trying to draw a dinosaur. And to think that I drew better with my feet than with my hands. Then she cut to the chase. "Don't raise your hopes," was her advice. "Emma and her boyfriend might be going through a crisis, but it's not over yet. She's really invested a lot in their relationship."

Common sense suggested she was right, but I was filled with a sense of omnipotence that made me feel invulnerable to whatever fate had in store for me. My heart had just emerged from its bunker and seen the stars in the sky: it had no intention of going back now, and the voice of wisdom was no match for its stubborn refusal to listen.

After the summer break, I returned to my old job in Turin while waiting to move to the new one in Milan. By the end of the first week I was already desperate to see Emma again, but I'd used up my money and had no idea how I could pay for another trip to Sardinia. I started to consider all the possibilities, including getting a lift on a fishing trawler, when my boss, Orso, asked to see me in his office.

"I've just read your interview with Michel Platini. The one where you ask him his views on true love—and whether he thinks it's true that separation weakens our feelings . . . Unpublishable treacle. You're yearning for your Miss Sardinia, aren't you? Of course I know who she is: she calls the office fifty times a day. Next Sunday your Toro is playing away at Cagliari, right? We won't send any correspondents, but I've persuaded the club to take you with them on the plane as an executive of their entourage . . . No need to thank me: I've only done it because that way I get the use of the phone line back. I hope you're not leading her up the garden path, eh? Remember: love is sacred . . . What are you doing, hugging me? Then you fancy me instead? Who's going to tell Miss Sardinia she's got a rival?"

Emma came to meet me at the airport wearing a headscarf and dark glasses like a spy, as if to remind herself that our love affair was a secret one. But as soon as she saw me she forgot all her precautions and ran to meet me in front of the cameras of a local TV channel who were there to record for posterity the Toro's arrival. Our kiss was broadcast over the entire island.

Two days later Miss Sardinia took me back to Departures. She was no longer wearing her dark glasses and her headscarf. She told me she considered herself my girlfriend and planned to join me in Milan in the autumn. She added that, on his return from his world tour, The Hulk was definitely going to split up with her.

She didn't say she would split up with him. But by now ignoring uncomfortable truths was part of my way of life. I wrote the classic Hollywood screenplay and played it out to myself inside my head: The Hulk comes back from his trip unchanged, Emma realizes she no longer loves him and sets sail for her new life with me.

Instead, The Hulk came back from his trip and offered Emma everything she'd ever hoped for from him: a house, marriage, children.

We argued endlessly over the phone, but it was an unequal battle—and I wasn't fighting it on home turf.

One morning in November, my legs like jelly, I entered the Palazzo dell'Informazione in Milan to sign my new contract with *Il Giorno*. I'd just hung up my coat when the telephone on my new desk rang.

"Hi. I just wanted to wish you good luck. You're beginning a new chapter—and so am I. I'm getting married in three months' time. Please don't get in touch again—you'd only hurt me and yourself."

I felt the same pain I'd felt in the Cubs' meeting room when Baloo had broken the news: an icy spoon turning in my stomach and hollowing it out—the looming shadow of death I'd spent all my life trying to escape from.

I went out into the street so my colleagues wouldn't see me. I walked across Piazza Cavour and along Via Turati as far as Piazza della Repubblica. A bench facing the traffic offered a refuge. I sat down and hid behind a newspaper. Tears trickled down my face, like drips from a faulty tap.

It was a pity the newspaper was a tabloid—too small to hide me entirely.

some difficult literary
moments followed

twenty-two

Some difficult literary moments followed, alternating between romantic despair and rhetorical posturing.

From this period in Milan I've kept a couple of written mementos. The first is Jay McInerney's novel *Bright Lights, Big City*, with its electrifying first sentence: "You are not the kind of guy who would be at a place like this at this time of the morning."

That "you" could easily have been me: a young man who's been dumped by the woman he thought he'd spend his life with gets lost in the Big City's nocturnal streets in search of himself, until he discovers that the real missing love he's never been able to come to terms with is the one for his mother, who had died of cancer.

The second piece of evidence belongs to the following

year and is the draft of a letter I wrote to Emma. Here's what I wrote, with some later remarks added in brackets:

Milan, 11th October

Hi Emma,

It's four o'clock, in the middle of the night—or rather in the morning—and I no longer know what sleep means. (McInerney's influence, all too obvious.)

I'm writing this from the landing outside my small flat. The colleague I share the place with has gone to bed leaving the key inside the lock. I keep ringing the bell but he must be sleeping with cement earplugs in his ears. (Did I want to make her feel sorry for me or make her laugh? I was describing some hapless wretch who couldn't even manage to get into his own flat.)

We left the editorial offices at midnight, copies of the paper hot off the press under our arms (as well as some nice female colleagues). (A pathetic fib to try to make her jealous. In reality all ten of us were men, high on adrenaline and ravenously hungry.)

One of us had been invited to go for dinner by a rival newspaper but didn't have the courage to tell the others, so he just suggested that we go on ahead and he would join us later in his car. Pity we spotted him at Porta Venezia heading in the opposite direction.

The restaurant was still packed and by the time we eventually managed to order our steaks it was already one o'clock. The food finally arrived at 1:30. On the bone and with all the trimmings. At two o'clock our Judas strolled in. He'd smeared his hands with grease to make out his car had had a breakdown. So we said to him: "You must be so hungry! But don't worry, you're in luck—there are two steaks left and a whole plate of chips." He tried to protest he had a stomachache, but ended up having to eat again from start to finish—even a meringue cake for dessert—at which point I thought he was going to explode. (The gall in trying to dress up coarse schoolboy pranks as examples of the "dolce vita.")

I miss you, Emma. Not so much for what you've already given me, but for what you could have given me later, when I arrived in Milan on my own, lived and struggled on my own, had to do all my own cooking and rely on the kindness of the concierge to patch up my trousers. (What I was really angry with her for was that she hadn't moved to Milan in order to cook my meals and mend my trousers.)

I've just had my birthday—my twenty-seventh, as you know. What you don't know is that La Stampa—*that's right, the leading newspaper in Turin—has offered me a job in its Rome offices. I'd like to talk this over with you. I've always wanted a lover who'd also be a friend and an adviser. I thought I'd found all three in you, Emma.*

I honestly thought I deserved you, after the kind of childhood I'd had. Do you remember I told you my mother lived in America, as the head of a multinational cosmetics company? (Since leaving school, I'd given my mother a series of high-flying promotions.)

Things weren't exactly like that—one day I'll explain. But I still thought you were meant for me. And that you too needed me. But perhaps I don't believe that anymore. (She'd chosen to marry another man, after all.)

I'm sorry, I'm writing a load of crap, and it's nearly five in the morning. The thing is—I thought you might need someone who'd write you a load of crap at five in the morning. (McInerney, again.)

I thought I could give you a world full of bright amusing people. As well as another world, smaller but also larger: just the two of us. A world called happiness, Emma.

Happiness is being able to make love at any hour of the day, so long as it's with you. Happiness is learning to grow together, being stubborn and quarreling, but still being able to move on, despite the knocks to our pride, to another higher phase of our love for each other. Happiness is agreeing to meet in a café and turning up late. (A strange notion of happiness.) *It's you being worried about something but the two of us solving it together. It's a bracelet I give you as a present, a shirt of mine you wash.* (After mending it, I imagine.)

Forgive me for these idiotic ramblings. I just wanted to tell you that I'm not missing the company of a woman. I miss you. You, who are a woman—and what a woman. But you're something more than that: you're the other part of me.

———

It's unfair perhaps to make fun of my old self. There's a dignity about real feelings which protects them from ridicule.

I wrote dozens of letters like this one. I even posted some of them, but never received even a postcard in reply—and there are a lot of nice postcards you can send from Sardinia. I've got one which shows the beach where we first made love. I had sent it to myself. Every evening I'd look at it and, after committing every detail to memory, I'd close my eyes so I could smell the sea and taste our kisses.

The idealized vision of Emma's face gradually faded, but never entirely. It took me two years to get over it—in other words to get back to feeling as bad as I did before I met her. Grief can open up windows into the self. It's just that I insisted on looking in the wrong direction.

The experience of losing love once again was bad for me. I was driven by a fierce desire to deny the past. I never replied to a letter—the last I ever received—from Sveva. Moved by a kind of self-destructive urge, I even stopped answering phone calls from My Uncle, the only person who made me feel I still belonged to someone or to something.

So I left to take up the new job in Rome—Rome, the great bitch who licks all our wounds.

twenty-three

I keep a round box in one of the bottom drawers of my desk. In its glory days it housed three layers of Danish biscuits, but a long time ago it was converted into a safe for a lifetime's worth of souvenirs.

Working up from the bottom, there's my first school exercise book, with the picture of a panther on the cover and on the first page the incipit which marks the beginning of my literary career: "Its autum and the leves are faling." Then my mother's frayed headscarf, the one with the white spots I used to flick against the walls when I played *tick-tock*. Then the worn pipestem I used to keep in my mouth after I'd given up smoking Camel Lights, whistling through it like a referee or a locomotive whenever I felt the need to inhale.

There's more: a photo of the vain Alessia at a fancy-dress party (she's dressed as an Egyptian queen); the note a girlfriend sneaked into one of my course books for Private Law: "However boring the lecture you're listening to might be, just think that this evening we'll be together"; the letter I never sent to Emma; her face in a Polaroid photograph: her fiery red hair has faded to a gentler rosé blur.

The objects from the time I spent in Rome are at the top of the pile: the first item is a cover from *Playboy* magazine with the photocopy of a Buddhist prayer stapled to it.

———

The Buddhists of Rome met every Thursday evening near St. Peter's Square, in a house which ironically looked out onto the bastion of Christianity.

It was a large gloomy palazzo which had belonged to an old noble Roman family. The lift didn't work, and the steps of the staircase were very shallow to allow carriages to drive up them.

There wasn't a horse-drawn carriage in sight when I first went (the service had been suspended some centuries ago), so I had to sweat my way up the stairs to the sixth floor. But climbing is good for the soul. After all, I consoled myself, not even Moses had taken delivery of the Ten Commandments down in a cellar.

As I slipped off my shoes outside the door, an organ-like sound took me back to the church services I'd been to as a boy. Here it was produced by voices chanting a mantra in unison.

Feeling suitably abashed in spirit, I made my way into the prayer room and, like the others, sat down on the floor in the lotus position, until a very unspiritual cramp in my calf muscles forced me to disentangle my legs and stretch them sideways, making me recline like a bayadère.

The leader of the group declared the meeting open. He had an unkempt beard resembling Che Guevara's and had probably been one of his followers in his youth, later channeling his revolutionary fervors on himself rather than society at large.

Each of those present then told the others about the benefits Buddhist practices had brought to their lives. The room contained a full spectrum of human types: the only thing which had brought them together was the experience of grief.

I was struck by their refusal to play the victim. A young woman who'd been a drug addict told us how at the nadir of her existence she'd taken to thinking that even the trees moved away from her to deprive her of shade. But prayer had restored her energy to live. She knew now that the causes of her troubles were to be found within her.

After each confession, there was a round of applause. There was also applause when a beaming university student told us that reciting a mantra had helped him solve the problem of where to park his car.

The applause, how to park your car—it was all a bit too much for me. But just as I was thinking this, Agnese decided to introduce me to the assembled company.

"He's got a problem with the father figure . . ."

———

I'd met Agnese among the alleyways of Trastevere, the winter after I'd arrived in Rome. After finishing work at the newspaper late at night, I would saunter off to join the company of the Eternally Hopeful—actors looking for a director, directors looking for producers, producers looking for money. Their tribe would move from party to party, terrace to terrace, succeeding only in eliciting a vague promise of "we must meet up for dinner sometime."

Agnese acted for a living but, more than that, she was an actress through and through. She was blond, sensual, unintentionally comic. She'd been in a successful film, had inspired adolescent fantasies by appearing once on a cover of *Playboy* wearing only a leather bikini and had tried out a whole range of thrills, with a marked preference for the most dangerous ones. She was about to turn thirty when an encounter with Buddhism saved her from the bonfire of the vanities and turned her into a soldier for truth.

It was the first time my bedroom has been used also for religious practices. Each evening Agnese would kneel in front of a small portable temple to recite her mantra. She always emerged completely refreshed from these intimate encounters with herself. She'd awoken my interest in the Buddha using that irresistible technique—a mixture of indirect allusions and doleful looks—women adopt when they want you to do something without asking you explicitly.

I took my time to say yes, coming up with nonexistent religious scruples, until I finally agreed I'd go along with her to a meeting.

———

"He has a problem with the father figure . . ."

"With the father figure? More with the mother figure," I objected.

"With the mother or the father?" the woman who took care of the incense (and who owned the flat) asked.

"I've got problems with both the mother figure and the father figure," a young woman, whom I thought I might have seen on TV, remarked.

"Me too!"

"And me!"

"You see? Here you're never alone," Agnese summed up, her photogenic face beaming with a wide beatific smile.

"But I haven't any issues with my father. I mean, I've got a few, but not important ones."

"Is that so? Then why do you always forget to pay bills and don't know how to change a lightbulb?"

"Do you have to tell everyone my personal stuff? What's my father got to do with paying bills and changing lightbulbs?"

"Haven't you always told me he's a very practical man? Your refusal to be practical is a way of criticizing him. It's your way of showing you're different from him."

"My problem is that I'm in love but I'm not happy."

I don't know how that remark came out. Perhaps it was Belfagor who inspired it—he'd seen the topic of conversation was bothering me and I wanted to change it.

Everyone's eyes turned on Agnese with a questioning

gaze. Except for Che Guevara's, who was looking at me instead.

"You've made an important discovery. Love isn't enough to make people happy. Happiness doesn't come from the world but from the way we relate to the world. It doesn't depend on wealth or health or even the affection another person feels for us. It depends only on us. We can all experience happiness. Let's repeat now: I can be happy."

A chorus of voices intoned: "I can be happy."

Che turned back to me. "You agree?"

"In theory, yes. But life isn't a mantra for people who are out to have a good time. We all have an intimation of the injustice that has been inflicted on us, which we cannot accept. It shows there's no such thing as Providence, because if there were it wouldn't have allowed it to happen. In order to endure the pain we've had to arm ourselves with cynicism to protect ourselves from the truth."

"How old are you?"

"Nearly thirty."

"It's the age when you first take stock. I know what you're feeling: I've been there myself. You feel as if you've been living on a downwards slope which has brought you to where you are now. As if you're the product of choices you've had nothing to do with but were made by the people around you. Was your mother difficult to deal with when you were growing up?"

"Yes, she was . . . quite difficult," I lied (but not much).

"My mother is a complete nuisance too!" said the student with the beaming face who'd solved his parking problems.

"You must learn to accept your mothers," Che Guevara continued in a subdued tone that made his words seem less peremptory. "Only by accepting your mothers will you learn to accept yourselves and to approach life without a sense of persecution, but with that vigilant nonchalance which is the secret of a life well spent."

"But how do you learn to accept yourself?" I asked.

"Each time you kneel down to recite the mantra you must try to reconcile yourself with your mother. Only then will you be able to see the truth as it really is, without the mists which conceal it from the eyes of the weak in spirit. If you want to change the effects, you must change the causes. Life will respond. It always does."

———

After that evening, all the questions which had been stored away in the loft came down out of their packing cases. Why did my mother have to die so young? Would I have been a different person, a better person, if I'd grown up as part of a loving family? Given that your mother is the first person who teaches you what love is about, was I destined to go on having to learn for the rest of my life?

Pray and you'll find the answers, Che Guevara had said. I prayed in Japanese, but the answers didn't come. So I started to look for them in books, in songs, in endless wearisome conversations with myself.

One night, after we'd made love, Agnese curled up inside my arms. I tried to synchronize my body to the rhythm of her gentle breathing. Before I spoke to her I wanted to make sure she was asleep.

"I want to be brave and tell you something—you, at least," I whispered into her armpit. "My mother died when I was nine years old. She did all she could to stay alive until the end, but she couldn't. And I still can't accept she died, you see? It's unfair, and I've still got to understand why. In those Greek tragedies you love so much there's always someone who takes revenge and restores the equilibrium that has been destroyed. But who can I take revenge on? On God who killed her and took her away from me? How can I, if I don't know where he lives or what he's like? And in any case your Buddha says that revenge doesn't restore equilibrium, it just creates new imbalances."

The morning after I woke up to a smell of coffee and Agnese's face smiling over me.

"I had a strange dream last night," she began. "There was a liar in my bed who was telling me the truth."

"Did you have a soft spot for him, a little?"

"I told him to stop thinking over things all the time and to start feeling."

"Good advice. And what does the chef recommend for breakfast this morning?"

"Something to set you on the right path again."

She handed me a tray. On it there was a cappuccino, a croissant and the photocopy of a Buddhist prayer.

We need to learn how to control our own minds rather than letting them control us.

My friends, let a new faith fill you. Keep polishing your lives like a mirror, day and night, never pausing to rest.

Learn to dominate your self, learn how to control with skill the reins of that wild horse, the mind. And then you will be free to run with the wind . . .

twenty-four

But I'd never learnt to ride, and the mind kept unsaddling me. I was too accustomed to trying to work everything out in my head to be able to surrender to the spiritual.

I sought refuge in the familiar world of work: that circle of journalists, politicians and intellectuals who choose to frequent the privileged milieu of Rome's airiest, most elegant terraces. If you want to avoid any possibility of self-examination, exchanging tidbits of gossip with the powerful is a sure-fire method for doing so.

And yet not even there did I ever feel I was one of them. I specialized in feeling ill at ease wherever I went. Among those interested in the spiritual life, my sense of the comic would surface, like a petulant little voice which prevented me from taking them seriously. Among intellectuals, I would feel trapped in their arid conversations, my soul parched and thirsting for the infinite.

There's nothing from this period in my biscuit tin. What can be found there, though, are the remains of a burst balloon wrapped round an old passport, the one with the visa stamp of Maybe Airlines.

———

A unique train of events resulted in my finding myself, in the summer I turned thirty-three, in the phone box of a military airport, wearing a bulletproof jacket and talking to my wife at the other end of the line. I'd got married four months earlier—but not to Agnese. Our love affair was more of a bridge than a landing point. No angry scenes accompanied our separation: we left each other with a sense of mutual gratitude and exhaustion.

I'd been rescued by a colleague who behaved abrasively with the people around her but was very sweet to me. She had read all my favorite foreign authors—in her case she had not needed translations—and at that moment was giving me a speed course in autogenic training on the phone.

"You're the most courageous man in the world!"

"I'm sorry, I think you've got the wrong number."

"Do you want me to call you a coward?"

"At least you'd be right. I'm pissing myself—and believe me, I am not speaking metaphorically . . . Look, I can't go to Sarajevo. It's under siege. There's no light, no water, no gas. People are shooting each other in the streets."

"I know, and I'm really scared too. But I also know you can do it!"

"And what have I got to do with this war? Three years ago I was still a sports journalist. And when I started to write about politics the greatest risk I ran was having coffee with some minister."

"That's just it: other people see you as just a humorist, only capable of seeing the funny side of things."

"I don't give a damn about what others think of me." I lied.

"Get on that plane and prove them all wrong!"

So with my goddess of war pushing me on, I adjusted the bulletproof jacket round my belly and climbed aboard a UN bomber plane full of food provisions. I dug out a space for myself at the back from among piles of tinned tuna.

The emotional high only lasted until takeoff, and was already running low when we approached Sarajevo, as the German pilot pointed out to me the Serbian antiaircraft artillery camouflaged in the scrub.

"If they shoot us down, tomorrow the United Nations

will issue a sharp protest," he told me in stilted English.

To which my reply, screamed in Italian, was: "What the hell am I doing here?"

The bulletproof jacket didn't protect me from a shameful fear of dying. I tried to fight it back by talking aloud to my mother:

"I'm a coward . . . Don't you think I am? Believe me, I'm a coward. The real problem is that it was cowardly of me to get married."

My tone had all the sincerity which comes at decisive moments.

"It's not my wife who's the problem. She's committed and determined—you heard her on the phone. It's me. I should have taken a climb, but instead I've taken a shortcut. I tried to change my life without changing myself. I told myself the fable of love between kindred spirits and the union of two solitudes. Then there's her family, which is stable and welcoming: a real family. Have I ever had anything similar, since you left us? But if I continue like this, Mom, I won't grow up. Even at our wedding I wasn't a bridegroom: I was the usual motherless child. I felt weighed down by shame during the ceremony. I feared the reactions of the guests when they found out you only existed in the lies I'd fed them over the years. Even though I have to admit your absence didn't seem to upset them—they seemed more interested in the buffet."

This self-examination session was carried out at altitude under the threat of antiaircraft fire: I was really pushing the boundaries of psychoanalysis.

"I'm still the same depressed elf who walks on tiptoe keeping his head down . . . Yet when I placed the ring on her finger, I thought I was looking at heaven."

The pilot and copilot didn't understand Italian and were giving me strange looks. Perhaps they assumed I was talking into a portable recorder? I doubt it. From the way they grinned, it would seem they thought I was mad.

"But perhaps, Mom, I only got married because I was scared. Yes, that's it. I was scared of losing something which I realize now I could easily do without—that illusion of stability and safety which is just a pale imitation of the sweet dreams you used to wish me when I was a child. Please let me land alive in Sarajevo and I promise you I'll make my marriage take off . . . I'll shake off all the old habits, immediately. I'll start again from the simplest feelings."

For example, by being nice to Matt, the Scandinavian UN soldier with a horned helmet who welcomed me to the airport, among dilapidated hangars and ghostly warehouses.

Well, "welcomed" is not the right word. He actually grabbed me by the scruff of my neck, dragged me heavily along the runway, out of range of the snipers and into customs, a mud trench with what remained of a battered desk standing in it.

Matt sat on the table and stamped the first empty page in my passport—Maybe Airlines.

"It's the entry visa," he chuckled. "Do you like the name? I invented it."

I gave him a cigarette in exchange.

"You don't want one?" he asked, taking a greedy drag.

"I've just given up."

It was true. I'd smoked my last cigarette during my honeymoon, on top of a hill we renamed Mount Respiration in honor of the occasion.

All the same I'd brought with me a multipack, on the assumption that in wartime health concerns take less of a priority. But the idea came to me of inaugurating my new life with a generous gesture. I turned my backpack upside down and a pack of ten Camel Lights tumbled into Matt the Viking's arms. He thanked me in his unintelligible language, but his smile was very eloquent.

————

Another example: being nice to Salem.

twenty-five

The hospital in Sarajevo floated like some phantom ship enveloped in clouds of dust, among blackened buildings and torn-apart streets. A nurse persisted in cleaning the floors with an inevitably dry mop, while a horde of mothers hardened by desperation pursued the doctors along the corridors and seized hold of their white coats, with pleas and threats.

It was one of those situations where even charitable organizations are forced to choose their priorities. The United Nations had arranged for an airplane to fly to London with forty children in desperate medical conditions. The doctors were going through the wards drawing up priority lists, which changed all the time because each day some of the patients died. A place had just become available, and all the mothers were fighting like lionesses, prepared to do anything to get their children to make progress on this absurd waiting list.

Room 51 in the pediatric ward looked directly onto the street since a bomb had made a hole in the walls and smashed out the glass in the windows. There were no more drips or clean sheets or food. Families crowded round the narrow beds. There was a bed in the far corner which had no visitors in attendance: in it lay a little boy with hair so black it seemed blue.

His solitude caught my attention. An ancient rubber pacifier protruded from his mouth, totally unsuitable for his age. A bloodstained piece of cloth on his chest rose and fell as he breathed. He was clutching a burst balloon in one hand.

I stroked his face. A shrill cry burst from him: "Mama! Dada!"

"He's calling for his mommy and daddy," said Doctor Joza. He was actually a nurse, but everyone called him doctor. He'd won his promotion on the field.

"Salem is an orphan. His parents died in a bomb attack a month ago. And then he was shot in the stomach by a sniper."

In other words, in that city there existed a human being who, because of some fatuous obsession with race, had hidden behind a parapet and taken aim through his gunsight at a little boy in the street playing with a balloon and had shot him in the stomach.

"Is he on the list for London?" I asked.

Dr. Joza shook his head.

"He hasn't got a mother to fight to get him on it."

It was as if a starting pistol for a hurdle race had fired in my head.

"I'm going to try and get him out of here."

I went round tormenting UN officials and British diplomats, but all of them already had their own lists. Out of politeness they added Salem's name to the bottom.

My last hope was the wad of dollars hidden away in my bulletproof jacket. I had to pay out a hundred in order to get a name—Commander Chuka.

———

An interpreter took me to my appointment through spotlessly clean streets. In Sarajevo the street cleaners stole a march on the war.

Like everyone else in the besieged city, we walked along one side of the street only, the pavement which was out of aim of the besiegers' fire. Every other step we'd look up at the roofs to check for the presence of snipers. Continuous bursts of rifle shots in the background accompanied us like sinister music. It was impossible to tell where they were being fired, or who was firing against whom.

Commander Chuka was waiting for us in a smoky bar. The walls were covered with student graffiti harking back to slogans of 1968. He'd been able to buy the bar from the proceeds of bank heists. In a previous existence he'd spent long periods in prison for armed robbery, but when the whole of Sarajevo turned into an open-air prison he'd dished out firearms to thirty youths in his neighborhood and proclaimed himself their leader.

What distinguishes the human from the inhuman is a sense of justice. Commander Chuka wasn't good. But he was just. He'd made sure the old people in the area got to safety and he'd fought a battle to get hold of a hundred kilos of flour which he'd then presented to a group of orphan children who'd taken refuge in a cave by the river. Every time he went to see them in his Mazda sports car, bright red and obviously stolen, the kids would kiss his hands, clasped to the machine gun he always carried round with him.

I told him about Salem and pushed a bundle of dollars across the table towards him.

"I'll take it, but not for myself," he said. "It'll help to oil the wheels."

I went back the following day, and he showed me a list with all the official stamps required. At number 11—my favorite number—was Salem's name.

Before I took my leave he handed me a red balloon.

"Give it to the little boy from me."

So it was that I entered the saddest hospital in the world with a smile on my face and a balloon tied to my finger.

I crossed room 51 and saw a crowd round Salem's bed. For a moment I hoped they might be Salem's Muslim parents, but they were fair-haired like the little boy wearing braces who was lying on the bed and gobbling instant mash.

Dr. Joza plonked a hand down on my shoulder.

"We've done it!" I burst out. "Salem's on the list! By the way, which ward have you transferred him to?"

"Salem died this morning."

I hugged the balloon so tightly to my chest it burst in my hands.

"Shall I take you to see him?" Dr. Joza asked.

"Thanks, but I can go on my own."

I shut my eyes and saw him. As a teenager, in his prime, as an old man—all the things he would never be—and then again as the little boy in the hospital bed, with a hole in his stomach I'd not managed to fill in time.

Once more I'd deluded myself that life was a story with

a happy ending, while in fact it was just a balloon filled with my own dreams and destined always to burst in my hands.

———

In Sarajevo I spent a month in hotels with no water and no electricity, meeting children who had lost their mothers, and their limbs, stepping on a land mine.

My own childhood drama was reawakened by those sights. It was the drama of my adulthood that no longer stirred any emotion in me. What earthly use was this life of mine which I was so scared of losing?

Before I went back to Rome, I helped the interpreter move some books out of his bombed-out house. I saw a copy of Victor Hugo's *Les Misérables* in French and looked for a sentence which I knew must be somewhere towards the end.

The protagonist Jean Valjean is dying, and his adopted daughter, Cosette, is begging him to fight to get better. She doesn't want him to die, but Valjean, a just man if ever there was one, reassures her.

"*Ce n'est rien de mourir. C'est affreux de ne pas vivre.*"

"Dying is nothing. What's terrifying is not to live."

———

Once I'd returned to my routine existence, I plunged back into my usual way of life. After a while I no longer kept looking up every few steps to see if I could spot snipers on the roofs of Trastevere. Even the memory of Salem began to fade. Belfagor had provided me with a shield of egotism and irony, and I hid behind it to avoid any sense of grief.

I forgot the promise I'd made to my mother. After a difficult year, my marriage broke down one evening, when my wife announced that her biological clock had sounded an alarm.

I stepped back against the doors of the wardrobe, as if to put a tangible distance between her impulse and mine. All my life I'd regretted not having a family. And now, when I could have had one, I realized I was terrified by the idea.

It's not really true that you desire what you've never had. When you're not well, you prefer what you've always had.

All victims have a tendency to repeat the old familiar formulas of the past. My past evoked Christmas dinners with Mita and Dad. Whenever I thought of a son, I never saw him as an heir, but as a potential orphan.

———

My protracted silence had worn My Uncle down, and he stopped trying to contact me. But while I was in the throes of my marriage breakdown, he told my father he would like to see me again briefly. He was ill and didn't have much time left to live.

We met in my father's apartment, where we had spent so many afternoons talking about the Toro, *tick-tock* and the books which only he had really read.

He'd lost all his hair because of the treatment he had undergone, but his eyes were the same, bright blue, like Mom's.

I should have asked him to forgive me and shown him unstinting love. Perhaps if I'd made such a gesture all my problems would have dissolved away. As it was, my embarrassment prevented me from saying anything more than small talk. I'd grown used to frequenting the terraces of the powerful in Rome and regarded my relatives' simplicity with ill-concealed annoyance. Thinking back on it, my behavior was disgusting.

When My Uncle died in his bed like Jean Valjean, his wife sent, to my address in Rome, a matchbox my mother had used to light her last cigarette before her final collapse. Someone had found it on a windowsill, and he had preserved it like a relic.

So I found out that on the point of dying from a heart attack, my mother had lit a cigarette. She must have been mad. Like me. But, unlike me, she was also good.

twenty-six

It was women who helped me out of the problems I'd got myself tangled up in, perhaps to make up for their mass desertion of me during my childhood. Everywhere I turned I was met by a smiling female face: the friend who found me a place to rent in her block, the cleaning lady who resembled the kindly babysitter I'd longed for as a boy, the bed companion who accepted me for what I could give her—very little, to be honest.

The rapid blooming and fading of my marriage had had a subtle knock-on effect on my sexual appetites. Sudden arousal would be followed by an equally rapid loss of interest.

Detaching myself was complicated by my victims' dedication. They couldn't get their heads round my emotional ups and downs. I was like those men who lack the willpower to leave the woman they no longer desire and allow themselves to be pushed out of the relationship as if it was she who was rejecting them.

After two years of getting myself into unspeakable messes, I made a decision to keep away from women in order not to ruin anyone's life. I drew strength from this voluntary abstinence. I began to feel I could survive on my own. One summer evening, convinced I was done with love for good, I accepted an invitation to a party on a Roman terrace. My life's soul mate happened to choose this occasion to come up behind me unannounced.

I was holding forth to a couple of friends on how not even the vulgarity of certain persons (I was referring to a colleague who had the habit of serving lasagna onto plates with his bare hands) could destroy my faith in human progress, when a glamorous voice sounded out somewhere just behind the nape of my neck.

"We're not evolved monkeys: we're fallen divinities!"

As I turned to see who'd spoken, I remember thinking: here's the usual crazy gate-crasher who's helped herself to a bit too much gin. Then I saw her and realized it wasn't only her voice which was glamorous.

After a silent appreciation of her fine cheekbones, I made the mistake of replying to her.

"How do you know you're right?"

"How do you know you are? The idea we've evolved from monkeys is just a platitude scientists have accepted because they can't come up with a better explanation!"

"And might that not be because a better explanation doesn't exist?"

"If you're using just your head and your five senses you're obviously not going to find a better explanation!"

"And what should I be using instead?"

"Your heart!"

My reader will no doubt have noticed that I was trying to advance through this philosophical jungle by waving feeble question marks in the air, while my interlocutor cut her way through with exclamations.

The girls I'd been talking to made off at the first sign that blood was about to be spilt. But in fact there was no clash between us. I merely greeted her revelations with a series of ironic grimaces and raised eyebrows.

Elisa told me about Atlantis, a civilization more developed than our own which had destroyed itself through excessive greed. Its ruin lay deep in the ocean, hidden from our eyes, but not from our consciences, if only we could use them.

I used mine and realized that this mixture of spirit and cheekbones had managed to dismantle the armor I'd worn so carefully all these years.

The friend who'd brought her to the party later told me she was his girlfriend. It took months for me to find out it wasn't true—when all I needed to do was ask her directly. When I finally did, by some kind of instinctive mutual agreement we immediately became a couple, almost as if we'd fallen in love with each other in some previous life—in an Atlantis attic perhaps.

———

I won Elisa over with an intimate supper at my place. She arrived under the kind of hat a silent-film diva might have worn, encased in a bright-orange woolen skirt which stopped at the knees to reveal a pair of jet-black tights disappearing into long boots.

She brought along two frozen organic pizzas, as if predicting what would happen to my ready-cooked veal roulades, which emerged from the microwave in a liquid state.

When a couple first gets together, you can see the purpose of the relationship in their gestures. Elisa came into my life to change the menu. But it wasn't clear what I was supposed to do for her. Amuse her perhaps? The expression on my face as I extracted the roulades from the microwave had sent her into fits of laughter.

When we went into the sitting room, I felt so much at ease with her that I decided to tell her everything. I don't mean the usual lies, but something quite amazing for me: the truth.

I placed an album of family photographs in her lap and sat on the arm of the chair to guide her through it.

"Here's me when I was very little with my mother . . . Don't say what everyone says: you were so cute: what happened to you?"

"I prefer you as you are now. I wouldn't like you with puffy cheeks and a curly head."

"But something really did happen to me. Look: my mother isn't in any of the later photographs. She died when I was nine."

"I'm sorry."

She brushed my hand with her long pianist's fingers and left them there.

"She was ill with cancer, but became so weak that she died of a heart attack on New Year's Eve."

She gave me a certain look, the kind of look a woman gives you when she's decided to trust you.

I tried to touch her knee with my free hand, but ended up digging her in the thigh with my elbow.

"The fact I've got no mother . . . is that a problem for you?"

She recoiled slightly, but more because I'd just managed to elbow her than because I was motherless.

"I know lots of people who are orphans even though their parents are alive—they've never been loved or understood."

"Are you scared of dying?"

Typical. I'm perched on the arm of a chair, waiting for the right moment to kiss the woman I might spend the rest of my life with, and I ask her if she's terrified of snuffing it.

However the question didn't seem to upset her—or startle her.

"I came quite close to dying when I was a girl. Since then I know what death is and I no longer think about it. I know it's a transition from one dimension to another, from the material to the immaterial. The ancient Egyptians called it emerging into light. When you think of it like that, it seems less scary, don't you think?"

"And what about life?"

"I'm scared by the thought of wasting it. If death is a journey, then life is the price of the ticket."

"Dying is nothing. What's terrifying is not to live."

"I think I've read that somewhere—I can't remember where."

"I wrote it."

If ever we shacked up together I must remember to remove my copy of *Les Misérables* from my shelves.

"Are you sure? And what did you mean exactly when you wrote it?"

I was beginning to understand the type of person she was. She wasn't satisfied with phrasemaking: she wanted to get me to the heart of the matter.

"Erm . . . that we need to confront life. That the suffering we undergo, the injustices, the tears we shed for a cause have a purpose. Though I couldn't tell you what that is."

"I think their purpose is to make us change. Haven't you ever asked yourself, when something bad happens to you: why has this happened to me, what's life telling me?"

"No, usually I just complain about it. And what might the answer be, in your opinion?"

"You'll make fun of me as you did with Atlantis."

"I didn't make fun of you! Not that much, anyway."

To prove my innocence I flung my arms out, like some arthritic butterfly, in the process digging her with my elbow for the second time, this time in the shoulder.

She took hold of my hands, in self-defense I think. We interlaced fingers and she squeezed mine. When two people fall in love there's no more beautiful moment than when you interlace your fingers in those of the other person and she squeezes them. A voyage of discovery is beginning.

I bent my lips down to meet hers, but I didn't have to bend all the way as hers came up to meet mine.

They tasted of sweet dreams.

the inevitable happened
to me without
advance warning

twenty-seven

The inevitable happened to me without advance warning, just as I was packing my bags for a work trip.

My father had been fighting for some time with cancer. He phoned to tell me that his condition had worsened, in the same dry bureaucratic tone he used to remind me to pay an overdue bill.

I felt my stomach clench. I was surprised by the intensity. Was I just scared of losing him or had I only now found out how much I loved him?

I changed the labels on my luggage and together with Elisa went to spend the summer in Turin, in the bedroom where my mother had spoken to me for the last time.

Dad was lying in the bed now. With the approach of

death, he was helpless, utterly unlike the man I'd gone in awe of all my life.

One August evening he watched the sun set through the window and knew he wouldn't see it again. He took hold of my wrist.

"You know I've only ever loved your mother, don't you?"

"I hope you've loved your son as well."

"I've never understood you. But of course I've loved you—on trust."

He tried to smile but was overcome by a fit of coughing.

"I still feel I'm to blame for your mother. If I hadn't gone back to bed and fallen asleep that night . . ."

"What are you talking about, Dad? I know you're Napoleon, but even he couldn't have stopped someone dying from a heart attack."

He seemed about to say something, but then closed his eyes instead. When he reopened them he was already drifting off elsewhere.

"After your mother died, you were too much on your own. I should have got you a dog."

"I'd have been happy with a decent babysitter. But don't worry about that now, try to rest . . ."

"Dog" was the last word my father spoke. I'd never heard him mention a dog before, and I attributed it to feverish ramblings. The world of animals had never attracted him.

The coffin was put on display in the sitting room where my mother's coffin had once been shown. Only, this time I was present, standing guard over the corpse.

As she passed by the refrigerated coffin to pay her respects with her husband, Giorgio, Ginetta took me aside and told me in an urgent whisper: "Sell this place. It's cursed!"

Her remark bewildered me. I immediately consulted Belfagor as to what it might mean. He put it down to Ginetta's grief at losing an old friend.

———

On my birthday, which also happens to be the feast day of the Guardian Angels, Elisa and I decided to take a walk up Monte Circeo, to try to salvage something of the missed holiday.

We were walking by the edge of the wood when suddenly, from under a bush, something completely white emerged. It was a dog, not much bigger than a large rat, with the muzzle and paws of a wolf.

He sniffed the air, uncertain which way to go. He looked at the various people out for a stroll and then headed resolutely in my direction.

I fell in love with him at first sight, so naturally I tried to shake him off. It's what I always do when I fall in love. I managed to leave him behind at a crossroads, but Elisa went back for him. She found him sitting in the middle of the road, waiting for her.

We called him Billy. Neither of us knew much about dogs—it took us a couple of days to discover it was in fact a "she." The name didn't change, only the spelling: Billie. Dad had sent me a four-legged guardian angel as a birthday present.

I would have been the first to scoff at this fortuitous alignment of the stars if it hadn't been obvious right from the beginning that Billie was a very unusual dog. She never barked at cats. Before she entered a room she raised her front paw as if to knock on the door. She cultivated her solitude assiduously and would spend entire days gazing at some undefined point in space.

Over time I think I've started to understand what she's seeing. She intercepts the energy emanating from love. She feeds on those vibrations.

If someone nearby raised their voice, that was enough to send her looking for a hiding place in some inaccessible corner of the closet. But if two people embraced within her signal range, they'd feel a light breeze round their ankles—it was Billie, the angel of love, happily wagging her tail with her tongue hanging out.

––––––––––

For work reasons I had to spend the entire winter in a service flat in Milan. Elisa and Billie would join me at the weekends.

One evening, when dark gray clouds filled the sky—and my heart, thanks to Belfagor—I took the wolf-rat from Circeo for a walk on a small oasis of green in the middle of the traffic.

The other dogs stood motionless in that patch of grass, paralyzed at the thought that if they sprinted off they'd be run over by cars. Billie, on the other hand, decided to entrust herself to the aerodynamic forces of her own small body and started to race frenetically round and round the small island of green. It was an absurd and marvelous sight. It was her way of facing down reality by transforming it into the dream she carried around inside her.

But Billie's lesson was lost on me. At supper that evening I sat facing Elisa, filling my stomach with ravioli and her ears with complaints about the world and why everyone treated me so badly.

"Why do you always play the victim when you're not one?" she broke in to ask. "The way you think is bad. And the way you eat is even worse. You're holding your fork like a chisel and you've got sauce dripping out of your mouth. It's disgusting!"

"My word, what sharp observational skills! So, Miss Twenty-Twenty Vision, the only thing which interests you in all I've been saying is the sauce on my chin?"

"Yes, it does interest me. A lot. You're forty years old and you eat like a spoilt child. Did no one ever teach you some good manners?"

"And who was around to teach me? Who? No one ever taught me anything. No one!"

I stormed into the sitting room looking for something I could vent my rage on, when I saw something white shivering between the sofa and the curtains—Billie.

She was terrified, but also offended: loveless as I was, I was starving her. I dropped to my knees and gathered her up in a hug which reminded me of hugs I'd received long ago. I started to cry—I didn't think I could. Billie licked all my tears away, and my anger gradually faded away.

The following morning I found a note from Elisa inside my jacket pocket. She'd written it on the back of a business card.

Remember at every moment that your mother is alive and is showing you how to live. She has always been with you. She's sad you don't believe in perfect love. Say hello to her when you wake up and talk to her all the time, about everything. She knows about love. Thank her for her love for you and make an effort not to give way to your skepticism. Just throw it in the wastepaper bin.

I would need to find a large one, but in the meantime I put the card in my wallet in the inside pocket of my jacket, adding it to the photograph of me smiling on my mother's lap and a rare example of my father's handwriting. On one occasion, at the bottom of the usual typewritten letter to me full of warnings about my unsettled bills and unpaid parking fines, he'd added, in pen: *Lots of love, Dad.*

twenty-eight

When I got back from his funeral, my godmother got in touch with me. Before reentering my life, she'd waited obstinately for my father to finish his.

She spoke to me as if I were a nine-year-old boy: she was still stuck in the past—like me, in a way. Our childhood affections are imprinted on our hearts, like indelible tattoos. They may seem extinguished, but they're only smoldering. And they are rekindled without the need for too much explanation.

My godmother turned out to be a survivor from a forgotten world. She came out of the mists of the past, my past, carrying a suitcase packed full with memories.

I was worried I wouldn't be able to remember it all,

so I asked her to write everything down—everything to do with Mom.

On Christmas Eve, she gave me a green notebook with squared paper. The pages were filled with a story written in a simple prose and clear handwriting, with no crossings out.

I got to know her during the war. I was working at Spa, a factory belonging to Fiat, which had just been bombed, and she had come for an interview. She was sixteen, three years younger than me. I remember her large blue eyes, full of anxiety and fear. I said to one of my colleagues: "There's a young girl waiting outside who looks like a little angel."

Sometime later I saw her in the office, wearing a black scarf over her hair. After she'd been taken on as a typist she'd fallen ill with typhoid and lost all her hair. Her fingers were blue, but that had nothing to do with her illness. It was the ink from the carbon paper she put into the typewriter to make copies.

We found out we lived near to each other and we started to meet up on Saturday afternoons. Then came the end of the war. The Liberation. The workers had occupied the factory while the women were sent down to the cellars for a whole day and night, waiting for the Germans to leave the city.

After we came out, your mother and I started to walk home. We had to walk in a zigzag, because it still wasn't safe. Fascist snipers were shooting from the roofs and we had to run. Your mother had a particular problem of her own. She'd broken the strap of one of her sandals, and every time we had to run down a dangerous road it would come off. I can't remember the number of times I had to stop and wait for her.

On the following days it wasn't easy for us to meet up, because she lived in Via Calandra, right next to two "houses of ill repute"—and the queue of partisans waiting to get in stretched all the way down to Corso Vittorio. Your mother only went out accompanied by your grandmother Giulia. She'd pretend not to hear the obscene appreciations of the young men waiting in line as she walked by.

———

Now that the war was over, that summer we let off all our past tension by going dancing. We used to go to the Pagoda, a dance hall on Corso Massimo, just next to the tram stop.

We would leave the office at five. The Pagoda was open until 6:30, and then again later on, in the evening, but I wasn't allowed to go out then. So we took advantage of that brief period before we went home for dinner to enjoy ourselves.

One table was reserved for Senator Agnelli, the man who'd founded Fiat. He sat there with his nurse. He would listen to the music without speaking, watching the young people dance. He was always the last to leave. He died a few months later.

On one occasion a group of elegantly dressed young men came in. We had never seen them before. One of them came up to the most beautiful blonde in the room and asked her to dance a tango with him. He said his name was Gianni. It was only after he'd left we found out he was Gianni Agnelli, the grandson of old senator Agnelli. All the other girls crowded round the blonde he'd danced with: "What did he say to you?" But she couldn't remember. Perhaps all he'd said was "Thank you."

Your mother wasn't aware she'd danced the tango with her boss.

When she was twenty she fell ill with pneumonia. Antibiotics weren't commercially available then, so the treatment consisted of giving her sulphonamide and applying poultices, but her temperature remained very high. Her breathing was difficult and sometime the catarrh was so bad she couldn't even swallow. The doctor who was treating her—well, he was just hoping in a miracle, like the rest of us.

Every evening, when I left the office, I would rush to see her. My mother was scared the disease was infectious, but she didn't dare to stop me—nor did she want to, really—from going to see her. She'd convinced herself that smoking got rid of germs so—to my amazement, she'd always strictly forbidden me to smoke—she bought me cigarettes.

But the pneumonia got worse, so I put on a brave face and went to see her head of department. He was a grumpy old man, but kindhearted. He called a senior person in the firm. The following day antibiotics arrived and your mother got well again.

———

She had such a sweet tooth. In summer she'd take me to a dairy shop near where she lived to eat ice creams. Once when we were there, a young boy came in dressed in overalls. He was riding a rickety bicycle piled high with goods he was delivering. He asked for the cheapest cone, but found he didn't have enough money even for that, so the woman behind the counter refused to give him one.

He got back on his bike crestfallen. But your mother called him back. I can still hear her: "Laddie, come here!"

Glaring at the woman, she ordered her to give him the largest cone available—whereupon she handed it to the little chap. She refused to set foot inside the shop again.

———

On our visits to the Pagoda she met someone called Carlo. He was a handsome lad—or rather a man, since he must have been thirty. In those days, when you were thirty you were a man.

Carlo was your mother's first boyfriend. He came from near Asti and owned a car. That counted for something in those days when everyone had bikes.

One Sunday he and his brother drove us to their hometown for the festival held for the local saint's day. The dance in the town square was scheduled to begin at sunset, after the evening service in church—too late for two city girls who had to get home in time for dinner. But Carlo wanted to dance with your mother, so managed to persuade the band to start up in advance. The townsfolk were all scandalized.

He was always out for a good time and never wanted to do any proper work. He took off before their relationship became serious. Your mother was very upset, but she got over it. Then there was Vanni, who'd left another girl to be with your mother—in fact, I think he married her after your mother got shot of him . . . I mean, ditched him. But she was never really in love with him.

She met your father at the wedding of two of our colleagues, Giorgio and Ginetta. Vanni had been shy, but he was completely different. It might seem strange to you, but when he was among friends your father was a real extrovert.

I imagine you know the rest of the story. How your grandmother Emma was against the match, the way they all had to live together in your grandparents' flat, the move to a new place and then your arrival.

————

Your mother was scared of physical pain. When her wisdom teeth came through, what a saga that was! They hurt whenever she ate, but she preferred keeping them rather than going to the dentist.

I'd offered to go with her, but on three consecutive occasions she didn't turn up for the appointment. The fourth time I went and fetched her from home and accompanied her all the way to the door of the dentist's surgery.

I rang the bell and said hello to the receptionist (we'd got to know each other well). I told her I'd finally brought my friend along. She said "What friend?" I turned round and your mother had gone.

I managed to grab hold of her at the foot of the stairs. When the dentist had finished taking the teeth out she asked to see them. She couldn't believe they'd been removed—thanks to the anesthetic she'd felt nothing.

———

Why am I telling you all this? I'm getting old and sometimes I forget what I'm saying . . . Now I remember: your mother was scared of physical pain. It was a kind of phobia which just overcame her completely.

The only time I ever saw her not paralyzed by it was just before you were born. Then she was so happy not even the fear of pain could touch her. I brought you home from the maternity clinic in my arms. Uncle Nevio drove very carefully—we were carrying a precious item!

Every Sunday afternoon we would come to visit and we always ended up staying on for supper, even if it was only some bread and cheese. While your mother did the washing-up, I'd lay you in your cot and talk to you. You used to like the sound of my voice—you would smile and start to complain if I stopped. What lovely conversations we used to have!

I remember once—you must have been about two—I called to say hello on my way home from the office and you flung your little arms round my neck, crying. You didn't want me to leave. But I think it was really because you liked the feel of the soft fur collar of my overcoat.

Some years after that—do you remember?—we'd all gone on a cruise together to the Canary Islands. Your mother was seasick and either stayed in her cabin or sat in a deck chair with me, asking what you were up to. You were always somewhere else. Everything excited your curiosity. You had a passion for the names of capital cities at the time. You would stop a passenger and ask him: what's the capital of Peru? And if he didn't know the answer, you would tell him off.

When we stopped at Cadiz, the guide who was supposed to escort us on a guided visit to a distillery turned up late. He didn't know Italian very well, so he said he was "sad" for his delay. I remember you were struck by the admission—and in fact he had a rather depressed appearance anyway.

When we got back on the coach to return to the ship, we found a bottle of liqueur waiting for us on every seat. You didn't hesitate—you took the bottle and gave it to our guide. "So you won't feel sad anymore." And in fact you succeeded in getting a smile out of him.

———

They were good times. But they came to an end when your mother became ill. I don't know what you've been told about her. But it was impossible not to love her. She was just such a nice person. She had a kind of energy about her.

After she died, your father told me we couldn't see each other on Sundays as we used to, because you had a season ticket for the Toro, even for their away matches.

But I was at work the rest of the week. I pleaded with him to come to some arrangement. He said that he wasn't accustomed to asking for charity: if I couldn't make time to see you during the week, then the two of you could do without me.

On Christmas Eve Uncle Nevio and I came to fetch you to go and buy your present together. You were waiting by the main door. Your father didn't even want us to come up to the flat.

I think he was jealous of my husband, who was a university professor and used to keep you spellbound with his talk. And then my presence must have reminded him of your mother at a time when he was hoping to close that chapter in his life.

How many times I tried to get in touch with you! But it was no good. I never cry, but one evening Uncle Nevio found me sobbing by the telephone. He got very angry and told me never to call your father again.

But I've followed you at a distance. Giorgio and Ginetta gave me news of you. When you wrote for Il Giorno *I used to buy it secretly. Then you moved to* La Stampa, *which we took at home, and I could keep an eye on what you were doing without resorting to subterfuge. For many years reading your articles was my way of being with you.*

We've met again too late. My husband is dead and I'm aware that with every month—let alone year—that passes my strength is not what it was and my aches and pains increase. But it's a huge consolation to know you're still around and that you're with Elisa. I took a liking to her immediately. Your mother would have done too.

Much love to you both, my dears—you're the most precious thing I have now.

Your godmother

twenty-nine

The final page was gloomy, but I closed the notebook with a sense of gratitude. I'd found out about the young girl who'd become my mother. And about how strong a friendship could be. Mom and my godmother had been like sisters—more than sisters, since they'd chosen each other.

I was struck too by all the things that little boy, so bold and energetic, had done. Had I really been like that once—before love and its strength abandoned me?

So the "if" game started again . . .

If Mom had lived, if she had been like any normal mother, I would have grown up with two women looking after me—my mother and my godmother. Instead of having to circle awkwardly round the girls I liked, I'd have gone boldly up to them and asked them to tell me what the capital of Peru was. And instead of spending my teens barricaded in my own room navel-gazing, I would have dished out bottles of liqueur to the world's depressed, at the risk of being arrested for encouraging drunk and disorderly behavior.

But it would have been all too easy. And what good would it have done me in the end? All things considered, I preferred myself having to carry a thorn in my side. I'd spent the first half of my existence regretting another way of life which, it turned out, I wouldn't have wanted to live anyway.

I still missed, terribly, the young woman with her blond hair and her hands blue from carbon paper and her wide eyes gazing at a world full of terrors. But I missed her in a different way. Now I missed the opportunity of being able to protect her.

———

I got married, for the second time, in the Rome registry office on the Campidoglio one spring morning at nine o'clock. We toasted each other with black currant juice. While I smiled at the photographer who was busy immortalizing the different poses we assumed against the backdrop of the Roman Forum, for a moment I felt like a man rather than an orphan.

With Elisa beside me, I was discovering new places and new books. I found that you can cultivate the spirit without having to belong to any established religion. I began to understand the secrets we refuse to acknowledge even though they're within us—or perhaps because they're within us.

I learnt not to surrender passively to events but to interpret them as signs. I realized that love can be a stick to lean on, but also a sword with which to conquer new insights into your own potentialities. For years I'd thought of love as something you acquire: now I saw that it involved giving something to another person.

———

I started to talk about such matters with readers through the medium of a lonely-hearts column. Elisa persuaded me to do it and to ignore all those men who think getting a sentimental education is a waste of time and regard any talk about one's inner torments as an admission of weakness.

One March day a particular letter arrived for me at the newspaper offices. As soon as I started to read it, I realized that life was finally presenting me with the opportunity to tell others who I was. I've copied the letter, as well as my reply, just as they appeared in the newspaper.

I'm thirty-nine years old and happily married. So I'm not writing to you about marriage problems, but because I had a wonderful mother. She gave birth to me when she was just twenty. She died from breast cancer during the Christmas holidays; since then my life has been like a black-and-white film.

Thanks to my mother I love the Rolling Stones (the Beatles too, though not so much) and Lucio Battisti— and mankind. She taught me to get on well with people, to show respect to those who are vulnerable, not to get upset when the world turns a blind eye and a deaf ear to romantics like us.

She worked in a factory all her life. Her love for my father was profound; she cared for my grandfather and looked after her own mother right up until her death, when she herself was terminally ill. When my grandmother died, she leant close to her and whispered in her ear: "Thank you for everything."

Three months later she died. It was a sunny morning. She could hardly speak but told me: "Don't you ever give up: you're a good lad. I'm honored to have you as a son."

I'm crying as I write this, but my heart is broken and I don't know how to get back to normal. It's just too hard to get over it. The pain is too extreme. So I wanted to write to you to ask if you, with your wisdom and experience, can suggest how to fill, at least in part, this enormous gap in my life.

Gabriele

Gabriele, I've got no wisdom and no experience. But I lost my mother too, when I was just nine. And letters like yours can still upset me, even nowadays when people go on TV to display their emotions.

Ten years ago, when I was thirty, I didn't willingly speak about my mother to anyone, not even myself. As a boy I unconsciously refused to believe she was dead. I hid her photo away in a drawer. If I can write about it now in a newspaper it's because I've learnt to accept my grief and to forgive, to forgive my mother for leaving me and the universe for taking her away—when she was only forty-three, after a life not so different from that of your own mother.

My mother's father died when she was a girl. During the war, at an age when today's teenage girls write and tell this column about their first boyfriend troubles, she was working in a factory as bombs were falling, in order to help her mother bring up her four younger siblings.

She was fair-haired, a bit harebrained, emotional—like me. She was selfless, always ready to help anyone, like a radiator always on steady heat. I wish I were like her in that, but I'm not.

If somehow she'd survived the illness which killed her during the Christmas holidays, just like your mother, I would probably have ended up today as a lawyer (that's what she saw me as—"He talks nonstop!"). Journalism is too risky a profession—I'm not sure if I'd have had the courage to upset her by going into it.

I envy you, Gabriele, because there's no mention in your letter of the most obvious recrimination: how could such a good woman go off in such a hurry? But your mother didn't leave behind in the nest some frightened little fledgling: she left an adult, and she had time to teach him how to love mankind, Lucio Battisti and the Rolling Stones—in a word, the basics of life.

But still, when your mother dies early it remains an injustice you just can't comprehend. What saves us is the thought that this life is simply an apprenticeship. We must get through it with a smile, if we can. Real happiness, however, must lie elsewhere.

We're here to prepare ourselves. But we're not all

at the same stage. Some are ahead of us and need less time before taking off the L-plates and driving away. If you're an angel when you're young, what's the point of growing old? That's not always the case, of course, otherwise only the wicked would grow old—and that's obviously not true.

So let's put it like this: each of us has a task to carry out in life. In our case, our mothers accomplished it more quickly than others. Because they didn't have so much to do, or because they were better at doing it. We live on as their sons with our memories—which, for you, luckily, outweigh the regrets.

I've been told that on the night my mother died the last thing she did was to come into my bedroom and tuck in the blankets. Your mother whispered those marvelous words in your ear.

Let's remember them like that, in the act of loving us and blessing us for the last time. And let's try to be worthy of them, Gabriele. Without showing off about it, without being scared.

———

I hadn't given a thought to what the effects of writing this might be. A warm flood of letters overwhelmed me, as if for a second my words had touched the innermost spirit of the world.

One woman wrote to tell me that after she'd read my column she'd gone to see her mother just to give her a hug. She hadn't done this for a long time, but she now thought herself lucky she still could after reading about those who'd missed their mother's embraces their whole life. The opposite of another woman, who wrote to say that, having lost her mother when she was just two years old, she thought I was fortunate, since at least I could remember mine.

Among my colleagues at the newspaper the revelation produced different reactions according to which office they worked in. The current affairs reporters who thronged the room known as "Tiananmen" pinned the cutting to the noticeboard. One of the clerks sent me his condolences.

In the room called "Capalbio," the office where the eggheads and the pundits hung out, and which I too frequented, no one showed any sign of having read it, except for one pointlessly pretty female colleague, who asked me which French film had given me the idea. Only a fellow columnist in her sixties known for her bad temper left two chocolates on my desk, with a note: "These are for you, with two kisses."

A very famous TV journalist called me to say how disappointed he was I'd turned sentimental. From a scourge of contemporary manners like me he would have expected more spice and less sugar.

He added that he was just about to go on a safari with a group of bankers. I wished the lions bon appétit.

how much time
had gone by

thirty

How much time had gone by since I'd made my public confession?

The blink of an eye, a mere nine years.

Billie had become even whiter and Elisa had grown even younger—her complexion was as fresh as a girl's.

I was working once again in Turin as in the old days when I had Orso as a boss—with the difference that I was now one of the bosses.

Belfagor had continued to doze on and off inside me. But the last few months had seen an increase in his activity, like a volcano coming to life which you'd mistakenly thought extinct.

It was writing my first novel—or the "novelette," as I fondly called it—which had woken him up. I started and abandoned dozens of stories, but I'd finally succeeded in finishing one. But the work of interior excavation which the writer, like an archaeologist, undertakes had roused my monstrous familiar from his slumber.

All those books I'd left unfinished proved how much the prospect of Belfagor's reawakening scared me. And yet, if I really wanted to change my life, I had to provoke him into action, tempt him out of his cave for the final battle.

The day of truth began with the Moka pot muttering away on the cooker without releasing any flow of coffee to break the tension.

Perhaps I'd forgotten to fill it with water? If so, there was a reason for it. My fingers were covered with bits of Sellotape: I'd been trying to patch together the copy of my book I had been hawking round with me in bookshop presentations, which in the course of its journeys had fallen to bits. It's a well-known fact that we men can't succeed in doing two things at the same time—after all, that's why we've created a society which allows us to get on with one thing only, leaving all the rest for our better halves to do.

My novelette was about a man who resembled me— he'd lost his mother too—but not closely. I'd sent him off to take the waters at a rather special health center, the Soul Spa, where he would be forced to undertake an initiation which I myself had never had the courage to face up to.

I'd made sure he was surrounded by spiritual doctors who knew Father Nico's favorite maxims by heart. I'd put obstacles and sufferings in his way, but at the same time endowed him with the energy to overcome them and to reestablish contact with his powers of intuition, that atrophied part of the brain which connects to the heart and enables us to hear what Jung called "the voice of the gods."

While I was writing the book, I'd heard it as well. It had shown me things which no chain of reasoning could ever have led me to, but which imposed themselves on my soul with all the force of a self-evident truth I had always known. Life sets each of us a test we have to face: mine was finding a way to sublimate the loss of my mother, to make up for the absence of female energy by discovering it within me.

Having put the copy of my book more or less back to rights, at least pending more serious surgical intervention, I put it in the bottom drawer of my desk, side by side with the Danish biscuit tin. Then I prepared an extra cup of coffee, but only had time to swallow it down in one go without even adding sugar: Elisa had appeared in the kitchen doorway with the car keys in her hand.

It was New Year's Eve, and like every year since we'd

got in touch again, we were going to accompany my godmother to visit Mom. At the cemetery.

———————

She opened the door to us with her handbag already
on her arm, but as I was helping her into her coat she
mentioned my novelette.

I'd given her a copy for Christmas, though it had come
out earlier, in the spring. The reason for the delay had
been an operation on her eyes—which had meant that
for several months she wasn't able to read the detective
novels she used to enjoy so much. I could have read my
book aloud to her of course, but the voice of the gods
had suggested waiting until she'd recovered her sight and
things could be done in the right and proper way.

I asked her if she'd liked the pages on my hero's
mother. This was the only part of the book where I'd
drawn directly on my own experience, although when
I came to describe her death I'd allowed myself some
poetic licence:

*She dragged herself towards the window . . . opened it wide
and held on to the sill . . . but her fingers were already
lifeless . . . they released their grip . . . and she fell forward*

into the void, her head upright and her limbs splayed . . .
she landed on a heap of snow . . . without a bruise or
cut . . . she'd died of a heart attack as she fell . . .

The image of the flying corpse had seemed to come out
of nowhere, as if I had dreamt it, while I was tapping away
at the keyboard.

My godmother had indicated to me that things hadn't
gone exactly like that. I knew that already. But I didn't
know just how differently.

"I'd like to give you something, dear."

"It's getting late, we need to get to the cemetery before
it closes. You can give it to me later."

I'm an expert in putting things off until "later." I
know every trick in the book for transforming "later" into
"never."

"No, not 'later'! You'll do it now!" Elisa intervened.

The lady of the exclamation marks will not shy away
from a problem: she advances towards it with an open
heart.

Emboldened by Elisa's moral support, my godmother
fumbled with dwarf-sized keys at the drawers of the bureau.
Her lovely, gnarled old hands drew out a brown envelope.

"After forty years, it's time that someone told you the
truth."

I opened the envelope awkwardly and took out an old newspaper cutting—from the newspaper for which I now worked.

It was the afternoon edition for the last day of the year, forty years earlier.

Madre si getta dal quinto piano

La tragedia all'alba in corso Agnelli - E' morta sul colpo, aveva 43 anni - Era stata operata di recente

Tragedia, stamane all'alba in corso Agnelli: una donna, madre di un bimbo, disperata per essere affetta da una grave malattia, si è uccisa gettandosi dalla finestra di casa. E' morta subito.

Si chiamava Giuseppina Pastore, aveva 43 anni. Abitava al quinto piano dello stabile di corso Agnelli 32, con il marito, geom. Raoul Gramellini, e il figlio Massimo, di 9 anni. Il 20 settembre era stata operata di cancro: da allora viveva nell'angoscia.

Stamane, sconvolta da una crisi improvvisa, si è alzata dal letto mentre il marito e il figlio dormivano ancora. Erano appena le 6, cadeva fitta la neve. Giuseppina Pastore ha aperto la finestra del salotto, è salita sul davanzale e si è lanciata nel vuoto. Il suo corpo è stato trovato nella neve, coperto di sangue, dai primi passanti del mattino. Uno di essi ha telefonato alla polizia.

Gli agenti, su indicazione di un inquilino, sono saliti al quinto piano. Hanno suonato a lungo, per svegliare il marito della suicida. Non si era accorto di nulla: sono stati i poliziotti a comunicargli la notizia del tragico gesto della moglie. E' rimasto impietrito, poi è scoppiato in pianto. Si è svegliato anche il piccolo Massimo; ma nessuno ha avuto il coraggio di dire che la madre è morta.

MOTHER THROWS HERSELF FROM FIFTH FLOOR

Tragedy at dawn in Corso Agnelli—43-year-old woman was killed instantly—She'd recently been operated on

A tragedy took place this morning, at dawn, in Corso Agnelli. Giuseppina Pastore, 43, mother of a little boy, threw herself from the window of her apartment, dying on impact.

She lived on the fifth floor of No. 32 Corso Agnelli, with her husband Raoul Gramellini, an accountant, and their 9-year-old son Massimo. She'd been severely depressed following a recent operation for cancer on September 20.

This morning, just after 6, as a result of a sudden panic, she got up while her husband and son were still asleep. It was snowing heavily. Giuseppina Pastore opened the sitting-room window, climbed onto the sill and threw herself down. Her body, covered in blood, was found in the snow by an early passerby, who called the police.

The police, on the advice of a neighbor, called at the fifth-floor apartment. They had to ring a long time before the dead woman's husband heard the doorbell. He'd been unaware of the tragic event all the time until the police informed him. He was stunned, then burst into tears. The little boy, Massimo, also woke up, but no one could bring themselves to tell his mother was dead.

thirty-one

In journalists' jargon you're said to have been "scooped"
when your rivals get hold of a news story before you do.
In this case my own newspaper had "scooped" me with a
news story to last a lifetime—my lifetime.

My godmother immediately told me the article contained a mistake. My mother hadn't thrown herself from
the sitting-room window, but from one in my father's
study. It was more secluded: she wanted to make sure that
no one would disturb her secret rendezvous with death.

My father had moved my desk to just underneath
that window when I'd had to give up my own room for
Mita and share both my father's bedroom and study.
He must have looked out of the window from which my

mother plunged to her death on countless occasions. How many times had I done the same, never realizing where I was, never knowing who I was.

———

I needed to feel alive again and went out onto the kitchen balcony to breathe in some cold air.

The article wasn't signed: it would certainly not be possible to identify who wrote it at this distance in time. Perhaps it was a cub reporter, forced to work the grave-yard shift on New Year's Eve.

I pictured him as he arrived, under the falling snow, at the apartment block where the tragedy had occurred, talked to the police, rang the neighbors' doorbells in the hope of getting in touch with Tiglio and pieced together in his notebook the story I would read forty years later.

Perhaps the reporter had been a woman—or a man with a feminine sensibility. There was a certain tact in the wording, even though the piece included details it would be unthinkable to publish today: the suicide's address, the nature of her illness, the name of the minor involved—me.

Any reader wanting to find out more about the pain

I was feeling could have come and rung the intercom.
But it was the afternoon edition on New Year's Eve: the
city was half empty and it was snowing hard. Only a few
people would have seen it.

————

I came back into the kitchen, placed the cutting on the
table and sat down opposite my godmother.

Elisa lightly touched my hands to give me courage.
I was about to undertake the most difficult interview I'd
ever had to do in my life.

"Why didn't you tell me before?"

"I thought you knew and didn't want to talk about it.
But when I read your novel I realized noone had ever told
you anything. I just couldn't bring myself to remain silent."

After forty years, the remark seemed like a joke.

"How did it happen?"

"She didn't fall off. She wanted to fall."

"She didn't have a heart attack."

"Your mother had a good heart, in every sense of the
word."

"So why did she do it?"

"At the beginning of the summer she'd had an X-ray,
and a shadow had shown up . . ."

My godmother's voice faltered. She took a sip of water to moisten her throat.

"The doctor insisted she should be operated on. We finally managed to convince her to have the operation in the middle of September."

"She told me she had 'things to do.'"

"After the operation she seemed relieved. She was a bit annoyed with your father. who had to leave Turin for some work-related problem."

"Typical."

"It was an excuse. The surgeon had told him the tumor was malignant. He took a plane down to Puglia to contact a healer he'd read about in the newspapers."

"Mom was in danger of dying?"

"The enemy had been defeated. The doctors thought there was a high chance the cancer wouldn't come back."

"So why did Dad go off in search of quacks?"

"Back then cancer was thought to be a death sentence. Your father was out of his mind with worry."

"My dad was out of his mind?"

"It happens sometimes, when you're in love with someone," Elisa remarked.

"But I still don't understand. If the tumor had been removed, why on earth did my mother . . ."

"The problems started when the doctors advised her to undergo radiotherapy treatment. It was routine, but she started to bombard them with questions. She convinced herself they weren't telling her the truth."

"But didn't she believe you and Dad?"

"She thought we were in cahoots with the doctors."

"She wasn't physically up to the radiotherapy?"

"On the contrary. Physically it was fine. It was her head that wasn't working. Every Sunday Uncle Nevio and I would come over and see you all. I'd go into the kitchen with your mother and she would start interrogating me. If she was undergoing treatment, it meant she still had cancer? Was nobody going to tell her she'd end up dying in lots of pain? If I was really her best friend—and she stressed the 'if'—it was my duty to tell her the truth."

"What did you say?"

"I tried to reassure her, to soothe her. I'd tell her off. I pleaded with her to fight her fears. I'd say to her: think of your son."

"And what did she say?"

"At least he's got all of you . . ."

And so I put the question which summed up all the others.

"Did Mom really love me?"

"For nine years you were her first thought on waking up and the last before she went to sleep. But then fear just completely took her over."

"Was she in pain?"

"No, but she was convinced she would be."

"Did she ever talk to you about killing herself?"

"People who kill themselves don't talk about it. Whenever I told her: 'Don't pull yourself down'—figuratively of course—she'd just stare at me and say nothing."

"You should have taken her away with you!"

"Where to? I invited her to come and stay in my cottage in Sanremo for Christmas. She just smiled at me sadly and said she didn't feel up to contributing to the holiday merriment. A few days later I got the telephone call from your father . . . How many times I've thought about her—standing on that windowsill . . . It takes some courage to throw yourself down from the fifth floor, you know. Courage and despair . . . The snow might have persuaded her to do it."

"The snow?"

"I'm sure the fairy-tale atmosphere with the snow must have made her do it. She must have thought that with all the snow on the ground the impact wouldn't be so painful."

"What about her dressing gown by my bed? Did Dad put it there?"

"No, I'm sure he didn't. He told me he'd woken up suddenly and found your mother in your room. She asked him to go back to bed, because she wanted to stay just a bit longer with you. Your father obviously didn't realize she'd come to say goodbye to you . . ."

My godmother passed her hand over her eyes.

"Do you need a hanky?"

"No, thanks. You know I never cry. It's just that I'm still angry with her, even after forty years. She had no right to leave you on your own. I always tell her that whenever I speak to her. And I speak to her every day."

thirty-two

It was too late to go to the cemetery now. We said goodbye to my godmother and left. The sky was the color of milky coffee: snow was on its way.

Elisa drove along in silence, trying to tune the radio to a channel for rock music. I twisted about, getting the seat belt—and myself—into a tangle.

My mother had refused to believe the truth and had killed herself. I'd put my faith in a lie and was still alive— but at what cost?

I asked Elisa to drop me off at my family's old apartment, which had been sold off long ago.

My eyes climbed up to the window of my father's study. I imagined a woman's silhouette standing on the windowsill, but I didn't have the strength to look at her.

I had gloves on, but I managed to take the newspaper cutting out to reread the last lines.

> The little boy, Massimo, also woke up, but no one could bring themselves to tell his mother was dead.

There'd been a slight misprint: "him" had been left out: it should have read "to tell him." And there was another, much more serious omission: no one had had the courage to tell me *how* she'd died.

The secret had been kept for forty years. The people who knew the truth had told me nothing. And they went on telling me nothing perhaps because they thought that in the meantime I'd found out from someone else.

Dad, my godmother, Tiglio and Palmira, Giorgio and Ginetta, Baloo, My Uncle, Madamìn, my primary-school teacher and who knows how many other people along with them. I felt I really should congratulate them all on keeping me in the dark so successfully.

Like Belfagor, they'd all acted for my own good. What might I have thought, at the age of nine, if they'd told me my mother had thrown herself from a fifth-floor window? That she didn't love me anymore. That I wasn't worth anything.

But the problem was that I'd thought this in any case, all my life.

So what would the right moment have been for me to discover the truth?

———

I turned my back on my parents' house and started to make my way towards mine, trying to find a grief within me which was no longer there or perhaps hadn't yet arrived.

The little boy, Massimo, also woke up.

That was something the reporter had got completely wrong. I certainly hadn't woken up.

I'd had forty years in which to spot the flaws in that absurd story: a woman suffering from terminal cancer who dies of a heart attack after smoking a cigarette. Yet I'd pretended to believe it, even though I knew the truth intuitively, deep inside me, to the point of dragging it out of myself in writing the novelette.

In an instant—a very long instant—I went back through my life searching for the clues I'd refused to see.

The two strange men holding my father by the arms next to the Christmas tree weren't doctors, but plain-clothes policemen who'd come to tell my father the news.

Nonna Giulia crying out, "What have they done to my

daughter?"—how could that have been about someone dying from a heart attack?

And then: the continuous references to the "tragic accident"; the tearful silences which sometimes overcame My Uncle; Ginetta's remark to me as we were standing by my father's coffin to sell this "cursed place" . . .

Dad. He hadn't even betrayed the secret on his death-bed. But I should have made him talk about it a long time before instead of avoiding the question with him and above all with myself.

I'd spent entire evenings in the newspaper archives looking for information on public figures and events. How come the thought of investigating the private event that had shaped my whole life—of leafing through the printed record for those days, if only for the curiosity of finding my mother's entry in the deaths column—had never occurred to me?

I suddenly stopped in the middle of the street to look at a little boy who was running along—and the answer came to me, as plain as a pikestaff.

I'd always known how my mother had died, but I'd decided right from the beginning that I didn't want to know. It would have been too much to take. Perhaps it was still too much to take.

As the years went by, the denial of the truth extended

to everything else. It attached itself, like a second skin, to my thoughts: it became my way of living my life while not living it.

That's what happens to those of us who carry a Belfagor around inside us. In order not to face up to reality, we prefer to live with fiction. We try to pass off the embellished or distorted reconstructions on which we base our vision of life as the real thing.

Many of the sayings we attribute to historical personages were invented by their biographers—and yet we go on citing them as if they were actually said by them. To reinforce our prejudices we prefer to read and to listen only to people with similar opinions. We lull our minds asleep with made-up stories and soothing versions of them, seeing reality as a myth and taking myths literally.

Our intuition tells us all the time who we are. But we remain deaf to the voice of the gods, covering it up with the chatter of thoughts and the din of emotions. We prefer to ignore the truth—so we don't have to suffer—or get better. Because otherwise we would become what we're frightened to be: completely alive.

thirty-three

Darkness had fallen. The streets were emptying, and the first fireworks were being let off early to see the old year out.

I'd walked for hours without eating, without speaking, without feeling anything apart from the the weight of my feet resting finally on the ground.

As I climbed up the last street home, I remembered My Uncle's advice and raised my chin as if I were stretching a string between it and my navel.

I was also thinking about my father. He'd taken it upon himself to protect me from the truth. The man who liked to tell shaggy-dog stories had thought up the saddest story of all and gone on telling it to me his entire life.

For the first time ever I saw things through my father's

eyes. I felt how much he'd loved my mother: the shock of it made me tremble. I saw him queuing up under the sun to call on that quack he must have despised. I followed him in his anguish as he went from doctor to doctor. My hopes were raised and dashed with his. Right up to that last dawn, when my mother persuaded him to go back to bed and he'd fallen into a sleep he would always reproach himself for.

After her death it was worse than being left on his own. He was in a desert with a little boy to look after. I would have gone to pieces in his place. But he lifted me onto his shoulders and started off again along the road. He kept tripping up and losing the way: he'd got the wrong shoes on; he chose inappropriate traveling companions. But somehow or other he succeeded in bringing me to safety.

He had really loved me. More than Mom. Because he'd stayed. The person who stays always shows more love than the person who leaves.

His masterpiece has been the construction of the myth of the departed mother. He'd inculcated me with the myth so that I wouldn't come to hate her, with the result that all the affection he deserved was spent on an imaginary woman.

The thought of my mother made me shake with anger,

but at the same time I felt an almost painful tenderness for her.

She'd been weak. No glory awaits those who escape their responsibilities.

That headline kept going through my head:

MOTHER THROWS HERSELF FROM FIFTH FLOOR

A headline always attempts to sum up the gist of a news report. Here what was important was not that some woman had killed herself, but that she was a mother.

That's what had really struck the reporter who'd written the piece among the printing machines, surrounded by panettone cakes that had done the rounds and colleagues wishing each other a happy new year as they hurried off home. That a mother had been so selfish as to sentence the child she'd brought into the world to a life without her . . .

In the hospital in Sarajevo I'd seen wounded women fight like lionesses against the approach of death, stretching their arms out in the crazy hope they could once more embrace their dead children.

I'd been in the room next door—alive. But that hadn't stopped Mom. She'd only thought of herself.

———

I got home. Billie avoided me. When I tried to stroke her, she went and hid in a cupboard with her tail between her legs.

I took off my shoes and stood barefoot on the sitting-room carpet. I caught sight of my mother's photograph on the mantelpiece, the one I used to hide in a drawer when I was a boy and which I'd always carried around with me as I'd moved from place to place—the one with the beatific smile I'd used to construct an entire myth.

I turned my back on it, only to see Elisa facing me. She too was barefoot: she'd come up behind me without my noticing.

"How are you feeling?" she asked. That question mark, unusual for her, spoke volumes.

"She wasn't the mother I thought I'd had."

"I've always thought of her like that. Like a jewel box full of passions and fears."

"Just think about it. Choosing to kill yourself when you've got a child."

"It happens. You're a journalist. Don't you read the newspapers?"

"I don't read that kind of news. I've always been turned off by it. Now I see why."

"If the child is really small, the mother usually takes it with her."

"I mattered so little to her that she didn't want me around."

"She knew you'd survive without her."

"Don't talk nonsense! She rejected me."

"She didn't reject you: she rejected life."

"But I was her life!"

Elisa stroked my hand in the way only she can.

"Her life, that's right. But your mother wasn't living in the real world anymore: she was possessed by imaginary ghosts."

"Couldn't she have been rescued?"

"Perhaps. She needed to be brought out from that world and back into this one."

"What could have done that? Or who?"

"There's no point in wondering about that now. What I'm trying to say is that fear always kills love. Even a mother's love."

We fell silent, looking down at our feet. Then she pointed at something.

"Your heels!"

"What about them?"

"They're on the carpet."

I lifted them immediately.

"Where else would they be?"

"You know very well: half raised."

"You mean I'm no longer an elf?"

"Perhaps you're an elf who's evolving."

"Evolving? Regressing, more like. While I was living a lie, I thought I could forgive her. Now I know the truth, I've realized I've never forgiven her."

Elisa raised her voice, as if building a dam to contain a rush of emotion.

"Stop playing the victim! Or the role of the injured son!"

"It's not a role! You can't just erase certain memories."

"But you can take the pain of them away!"

"How?"

"By learning to forgive—that's how!"

"How do you know?"

"Only by forgiving can you make contact with the energy of love again. I've experienced that many times. And I've read it in many books. Yours included."

"But how can you forgive a deserter?"

"It's obvious you've never suffered enough to want to die. It takes an extraordinary willpower to get up every day with the thought that life is an ordeal which you must face even when you're sure you're the victim of a terrible injustice and you're scared you're not going to make it."

"So now it's an act of heroism to choose to live!"

"Of course it is! A constant act of heroism. Your mother decided to give up. Just as you have, in a way. Since you refuse to face reality."

"What does that mean?"

"Ever since you were a little boy, you've lived with the same monster who killed your mother. But now you must defeat it, otherwise your mother's sacrifice will have been pointless."

A silence fell on the room—so deep it seemed to absorb the intensifying explosions of the fireworks. Then, as if from some mysterious cave, I heard the sound of my own voice emerging.

"What was she thinking about when she stubbed out her cigarette, took off her slippers and climbed onto the windowsill? As she stood there balancing, breathing in the snow before leaping off? While she was falling, at least, would she have thought about me?"

"Is it so important?"

I turned round to look at my mother's photograph and saw it as if for the first time.

"No, it isn't. Not anymore."

"Get rid of the weight round your heart, Massimo. You've tormented yourself—and your mother—your entire life over this. I've felt it hanging over us all the time we've been together. It's time to stop! Give her your love and let go of her at last . . ."

Outside, the snow was beginning to fall. Elisa's hands moved inscrutably round my head, and her voice uttered words I could not comprehend. But someone inside me understood perfectly what they meant: Belfagor.

I felt him shrink inside me like a shriveled sponge and then disintegrate into a dust of particles immediately swallowed up by the dark.

I closed my eyes and saw Mom come into the room where a little boy was fast asleep.

She sat down on the edge of the bed and looked at me for a long time in silence. She stretched out her hand to stroke me, but soon withdrew it so as not to wake me.

She tucked the blankets in, leant over me and whispered something in my ear.

Sweet dreams, little one

At that moment I smelt the fragrance of her hair and felt all the energy within her leave her body and penetrate my heart.

She stood up, took off her dressing gown, folded it

carefully and placed it at the foot of the bed. Then she went towards the light.

I wished her a safe journey; I opened my eyes and I put my arms round Elisa.

I don't know how long we stayed like that. But at a certain point I felt life rising up like a fresh breeze blowing round my ankles.

I looked down and there was Billie, wagging her tail— light as a feather.

acknowledgments

All the names in the book are the real names of the persons involved. I have changed only the names of the girlfriends, apart from Elisa, who is Elisa.

My main debt of gratitude goes, as always, to her. But this time the list of people to thank is a long one, starting with Giuseppe: it is in his office that the idea for the book took shape.

I'd gone to see my publisher, Longanesi, to discuss plans for my next book. It was going to be about how we might begin to dispel the attitudes of inertia and resignation—a result of our fears—with which we seem to face the present historical situation. The title would be: *Nessun dorma.*

In order to make the moral high horse a bit sturdier,

I'd thought of adding, by way of a preface, a short autobiographical piece explaining how I had dealt with my mother's death. While I was telling the story to Giuseppe some colleagues from the editorial team—Alessia, Fabrizio, Guglielmo—came into his office. By the time I'd finished, there wasn't a dry eye among them. Seeing their reactions I realized this wasn't the preface to another book but a book by itself, the history which had been developing inside me for forty years.

The moment had come to confront it and bring it out into the open—to turn it into a book, a novel made up of facts which had really happened.

I drafted the plan of the book overnight, and the writing of it was also unusually fast. The work—every day over three weeks—was visceral: I drew the story out of myself like copying out from a tape recording. Then I spent six months rereading it—a hundred, two hundred, perhaps three hundred times, adding and cutting each time, making continual adjustments like some psychoanalytical tailor.

Throughout the work, I was helped a lot by chewing vitamin C tablets (writing about my mother brought on a continual sore throat), Mozart's piano concertos in Daniel Barenboim's recording and the brilliant team of colleagues I've now been working with for years:

Stefano, Cristina, Luigi, Valentina, Alessia, Elena and, of course, Giuseppe and the courteous but ruthless Guglielmo. I've kept the text messages they sent me after they'd read the first draft of *Sweet Dreams*. They'll bring it luck.

I forgive the people mentioned in this story who've done me harm, and I apologize to those I have harmed.

A special thanks must go to my godmother, the *dea ex machina* of the story. If this has taken its present form, then the merit (or blame) must be shared equally between me and her, as well as between the team at Longanesi and the parallel team of friends who contributed with their suggestions.

1. Piula, Arianna and Arnaldo, who persuaded me to rewrite a couple of chapters.

2. Fede, who advised me to remove some unnecessary flourishes.

3. Marco, who cheered me on so that I'd expand the scenes to do with the Toro and with Dad.

4. Annalaura, who's in the *biscuit* tin.

5. Gabriele, who was moved.

6. Irene, who was amazed.

7. Francesca, who wanted more song titles.

8. Duilio, who wanted the book to be called *The Photo in the Drawer*.

9. Mirella, who whenever she calls me is always convinced she's talking to a writer.

10. Alexandra, who read the book up in the air.

11. Fabio, who read it while the snow was falling.

12. Annalena and Mattia, who read it and together arrived at the heart of it.

That makes twelve, my favorite number.

Turin, January 2012

sweet dreams and after

I've managed to write one of those books that change your life. The day after I went on television to talk about it, I had to be taken to hospital. I had a temperature of forty and an infection in my lower abdomen which made me howl like a werewolf.

Yet the evening before I felt fine. While getting ready in the dressing room for a TV interview I'd met one of my idols, the head of Equitalia, the Italian equivalent of HMRC. He's a noble and sensitive soul trapped behind a villain's mask. The schedule for that evening's program was really upbeat: an interview with him on taxes followed by one with me on what it's like to be an orphan.

After regurgitating, on live TV, the bitter memories of my childhood, I left the TV studio visibly affected by the ordeal. On my way out I found the passage blocked by a line of huge policemen loaded with guns. My performance must have gone even more badly than I thought, seeing they'd already come to get me.

I was looking round for an escape route when the Rambo-like bodyguards parted like the Red Sea and the Moses of the nation's tax returns appeared in the middle. He'd been crying, and his glasses had steamed up. Seeing the sobbing face of a man who's more used to making others shed tears is—believe me—a moving experience.

He came up to me and wagged his finger in admonishment: "Just remember, Gramellini, I've got my eye on you!" In order to reassure him, I swore by all I held most sacred—the Holy Inland Revenue and the blessed Annual Tax Return—that I too would soon be weeping and shell out tax on royalties till my last breath.

———

The next day I noticed people giving me commiserating smiles as I walked along the street. I didn't understand why, but I smiled back. It was only when a woman came up and stroked my cheek that I realized something was up. But I didn't have time to work out what it was, since I had to be rushed off to the hospital that same afternoon. After examining me, the doctor said: "So it's true that TV is bad for you."

He sent me home clutching a long list of antibiotics I had to buy at the chemist's. As a practicing homeopath, I obeyed with great reluctance. I see having to swallow down any chemical substance as an intrusion. I went and got the prescriptions and paid with a fifty-euro note, but instead of handing me my change the lady pharmacist behind the counter gave me a queer look and holding the banknote up to the light asked me sharply: "Are you Gramellini?"

It was one of those existential questions that put you on the spot.

"Please come with me a moment."

I wobbled after her on weak legs, passing a line of customers waiting to hand in their prescriptions. They cast disapproving glances. One old lady murmured: "They go on the box to tell others how to behave and then they try to pay for things with counterfeit notes. What is this world coming to?"

Once we got to her office, the pharmacist changed expression. She became a picture of mournfulness. She looked at me as if she'd found her long-lost twin, or as if we belonged together: she was the sacrificial roast lamb while I was the roast potatoes (somewhat burnt). She stroked my beard, offered me a mint to suck and wept on my shoulder (not necessarily in that order). Then, completely ignoring my groans of pain, she started to tell me about her family.

She'd had a highly strung daughter who'd taken leave of existence by downing a bottle of bleach—and a grand-daughter who'd been told a lie about her mother's death when she was little—"Your mom ate some contaminated fish by mistake"—and who was now a fifteen-year-old anorexic who refused to eat food because she associated it with dying.

The pharmacist offered me another mint.

"What should I do? Should I tell her the truth and risk making the situation even worse? Please tell me what you think I should do, Mr. Gramellini . . ."

––––––––––

And that was just the beginning. From that day onwards, hundreds of stories of sick and unhappy lives poured down on me. I was the pharmacist they were queuing up to see.

I think it's called empathy. People see themselves reflected in a true story, disguised as a novel but without a trace of reticence, and it's a green light for them to respond by telling their own stories. Not to their nearest and dearest, but to the friend they've met on the pages of his book, the companion they've found for the ups and downs they've experienced in their own lives.

I was told all kinds of stories. Despite the bleak subject, some of them were even entertaining. A friend I'd known in my teens wrote to me: "Just like you I found out a family secret by coming across a newspaper article." And he told me how, when he'd had to do some research in the archives for some court case he was preparing, he'd come across a file with his surname on it. Inside he'd found a yellowing newspaper cutting from which he learnt that his father—who'd been universally regarded as the most upright and honest of men—had been sentenced to prison when he was a young man for theft. No one had ever had the courage to tell his son. "And yet," he wrote, "I knew subconsciously. Now I'm able to confess it to you, Massimo. As a boy I was a kleptomaniac. Do you remember those skis of yours which mysteriously went missing?"

Didn't I just! I'd left them for a moment propped up outside the chalet when I went to have a pee and came back to find them gone.

"I stole them," my friend confessed to me (about thirty years after he took them). "Then I sold them. But I also want to let you know that I gave the proceeds to charity."

Another letter arrived postmarked from a holiday resort which years before had been in the news because a fire had broken out in a hotel where the hotel's owner had ended up dying.

The writer of the letter told me that the owner had been his father. He'd made sure, by inventing some excuse, that all the guests and staff had left the building, then he'd set fire to the wooden walls and gone up to the attic to wait for the end to come.

A few months later his mother had died of a broken heart. My pen pal found himself on his own with his entire life in ruins around him. He'd used his father's savings to rebuild the hotel in the same place where it had formerly stood. In this work of rebuilding his life—not just the hotel—he'd had a girlfriend. But as soon as life seemed to be getting back to normal, Belfagor piped up.

In my novel, Belfagor is the name I gave when still a boy to the monster who lives inside us—an ugly spirit who seemingly has our best interests at heart, but is in reality a pernicious influence. In order to protect us from suffering, he shuts us up in a cage of fears: fear of living, of loving, of believing in your own dreams.

The writer of the letter convinced himself he had to

leave his girlfriend. With the typical cowardice shown by men when they want to dump a woman, he didn't have the strength of character to leave her himself. Instead, he did everything he could to make her decide to leave him—and after prodigious efforts he succeeded.

He'd been given a copy of *Sweet Dreams*, but didn't open it for a month. He left it on his bedside table. It scared him. "But one night," he wrote in the final part of his letter, "one night I tossed and turned like some fish caught in a net, so I switched on the light and started to read through the book. I got as far as the final chapter—the one where Elisa teaches you how to forgive and how to accept life for what it offers us—and I realized the book was talking directly to me. It was nearly dawn outside. I closed the book and put a sweatshirt over my pajamas and went out to stand under the apartment block where my girlfriend lived. I buzzed the intercom, and she put her head out to see who it was. I shouted: 'Will you take me back?' She didn't reply: she just opened the front door to let me in."

With *Sweet Dreams*, I opened a door through which compliments, confessions and thanks have poured in—thousands of expressions of gratitude, by post, via email and on social-networking sites—raising a useful wall to lean against when things don't go well. For the open door also let in some people who wanted to give me a slap on the face rather than a compliment.

It was to be expected. If you lift the veil on your innermost torments, you risk being attacked by those who find such sincerity unbearable—because they fear they might be infected by it. A few people wrote to tell me I'd wanted to make money out of a family tragedy; others criticized me for exploiting the public's morbid interest in my private life, as if I were some kind of football star or groupie.

So, if I knew from the start the risks I was running in publishing such a novel, what made me do it? That's easy to answer. When destiny provides you with a story to tell and the tools with which to tell it, it's not right you should keep it to yourself.

For a long time I'd wanted to remind my readers that life has a meaning and that we shouldn't let ourselves become paralyzed by thinking about all the "ifs" and "might have beens." On the contrary, we need to face up to life "in spite of." As George Bernard Shaw put it: "This is the true joy in life . . . the being a force of Nature instead of a feverish selfish little clod of ailments and grievances complaining that the world will not devote itself to making you happy." Yet there are certain messages which come across as false if they're seen as being spoken by a journalist regarded as one of the privileged elite. Only a ruthlessly frank confession of my own misfortunes and my own weaknesses would make the message/massage of hope I wanted to give believable.

———

Losing my mother at such an early age, I'd experienced in advance the trauma which sooner or later strikes all of us. The loss of love.

In *Sweet Dreams,* I wrote that we suffer when we're not loved, but it's a worse suffering when we're loved no longer, when we feel like a moldy sweet someone has tasted and spat out. It's the fear of being abandoned which prevents us from abandoning ourselves.

When I mention these ideas in public, I always get puzzled looks. So I tell the audience they come from Jung.

In order to stop being frightened of suffering, we need to free ourselves from pain. Millions try to do this every day, pouring their efforts into prayers and good works or trying to stun themselves with drugs or other extreme experiences. But, as Jung said, you can't just eliminate painful memories. What you can eliminate is the pain associated with those memories.

Nowadays I can think of my mother without feeling pain, because in my innermost self I've learnt how to acknowledge an undemonstrable truth: everything that happens to us is always just and always perfect. Pain doesn't happen to us because we're unlucky: it's the opportunity we're offered to recognize the unresolved part of ourselves.

Why do we like hearing or reading stories so much? Because stories reveal to us, as in a cipher, the secret of existence. At the beginning of a story the protagonist doesn't know who he really is. He has a dream, but denies its existence or doesn't even realize he's got one. So it's up to the narrator to play the part of the laws governing the universe—or God, if you like—and subject the hero to a series of challenges which will allow him to reveal to others, as well as to himself, who he really is. If your life doesn't change completely—or at least in part—between your being born and your coming to die, that's tantamount to saying you've lived all the years of your life for nothing.

———

When I was a boy I was given a T-shirt with a phrase printed on it. It was supposed to be something King Arthur had once said to the knights of the Round Table: "We've been forced to go round the world in search of adventures because we were no longer capable of going on adventures in our own hearts." The phrase was a revelation to me. So the heroic exploits the world applauded were nothing more than pale imitations of the real adventure, the one each of us can undertake within ourselves.

Today's society is incapable of conceiving great adventures. It drags itself along in a suffocating present, poisoned by the fear of losing what it has, including the things it could perhaps do without. It exalts the lowest emotions, to the point that a marvelous word like "detachment" has come to have only negative connotations. It despises feelings.

Emotions are violent and short-lived: they overcome you and then they disappear. Feelings on the other hand are slow and deep. Sometimes they're boring. Yet they speak the universal language of the heart, which isn't a language made up of words or reasonings, but of symbols. It's the language of music, of myth, of fairy tales. And it uses the shrunken muscle of our intuition to communicate with us: what Jung called "the voice of the gods."

The voice whispers continuously to us what we should do. It tells us when a person or a choice is right for us and when it isn't. It reminds us that life has a meaning, always, even when we don't like the meaning. An authentic revelation our hearts are ready to acknowledge, in spite of Belfagor's efforts to make us believe it's merely a consoling illusion.

Intuition cannot lie and cannot err. But in order to hear it, we have to stop covering up its voice with the noise of thoughts and emotions. The problem is that it so puts the wind up Belfagor he'll think up any ruse to prevent us listening to it—rounds of applause at funerals, for example.

———

Our brain knows everything, but it prefers to pretend it doesn't know. For forty years mine concealed the truth of my mother's death and let me believe the story made up by my father, a man who was so steeped in real life he'd never bothered to read a novel.

Our bookcases at home were filled with rows of history books, but there wasn't a single work of fiction in them. I grew up surrounded by biographies of Napoleon. My father hero-worshipped the Emperor of the French and hoped I'd resemble him—not only by being bald.

One day I gave him *War and Peace* to read.

"Yes, it's a novel," I said, adding quickly: "but it's all about Napoleon."

To please me he started to read it, but after a hundred or so pages he gave up.

"Look, here it says that at such and such a time in such and such a place Napoleon was at this encampment. But that isn't true: he was somewhere else thirty miles away!"

"Dad, it's a novel . . ."

"And so what? This Tolstoy of yours should have done his research before writing such rubbish!"

So no more *War and Peace* or any other novel for him. And yet . . . to protect his son he made up his own about my mother's death—which I was the only person to believe was true.

The other people who knew what had really happened never said anything to me—when I was little because they thought it wasn't the right thing to do, and when I'd grown up because they assumed that in the meantime someone else had told me and I didn't want the subject raised.

Perhaps that could only happen in a city like Turin, where people are reserved. In Rome, sooner or later, someone would have leant out of a window and shouted, "Come on, Max, wake up a bit . . . ," and told me why.

Well, maybe. Who knows? What I'm trying to say is that even if no one ever told me, inside me I knew everything. I ignored the voice of the gods which was whispering the truth to me.

———————

Did I want to know the truth? Perhaps not when I was nine. But I'd certainly have liked to find out before I was forty-nine.

It's vital to be told about evil. But it's also dangerous. In the long run it can make us cynical or plunge us into despair, because we become convinced the world is a place of immutable horror. For this reason I prefer to tell the tale of good alongside that of evil—by telling stories about the people who've courageously stood up to evil and managed to defeat it because they've never stopped believing the world can be transformed by dreams.

Only the dreamer of wonderful dreams can draw on the energy of the universe—in other words, love. But we no longer have wonderful dreams. We no longer conjugate verbs in the future tense. And when the future disappears, the first thing to die along with it is the present.

Haven't you noticed how the only people who still think about the future are people in love? Have you ever listened to the way they talk? Have you ever listened to the way you talk when you're in love? People in love are continually making plans because they're in touch with love's energies. When you're prey to passion, of whatever kind, you're possessed by its energy.

So I advised the pharmacist to tell the truth to her granddaughter: her mother had eaten a dream full of poison because she'd lost contact with love. And the truth needed to be accepted and remembered without grief, filling the table each day with good dreams, nourishing and easy to digest.

So I reassured my kleptomaniac friend that he shouldn't feel guilty about stealing my skis, only acknowledge that it was a wrong action for which he'd amply compensated through the generosity of his friendship.

And so I wrote back to the young hotelier to tell him that suffering had shown him the power of love—that the girlfriend who had waited for him and forgiven him hadn't done it out of weakness. On the contrary, her strength was such she'd kept her own dreams intact in spite of the indecisiveness of the man she loved. She knew that "if you've got a dream and it's your dream, the thing which you've come into the world to do, you can spend your entire life trying to hide the fact under a cloud of skepticism, but it will never let go its hold on you. It goes on sending out desperate signals—like boredom and lack of enthusiasm—in the hope that sooner or later you'll rebel."

That's not Jung. It's me. And William Shakespeare said it too, long before me and much better. It's the summer solstice, midsummer night. Sweet dreams, everyone!

—Massimo Gramellini, Rome, June 21, 2012

about the author

Massimo Gramellini is deputy editor at *La Stampa,* where he runs a front-page daily column. A household name in Italy, he is the author of several books, including *L'ultima riga delle favole (The Last Line of Fairy Tales)* and *Fai bei sogni (Sweet Dreams),* an international bestseller that has been translated into fourteen languages.

about the translator

Stephen Parkin is Curator, Italian Studies, at the British Library, with responsibility for the Library's early printed Italian collections (1501–1850). His published translations include Giuseppe Garibaldi's *My Life* (2004), Edmondo De Amicis's *Constantinople* (2005), Roberto Olla's *Il Duce and His Women* (2011) and Giuseppe Tomasi di Lampedusa's *Childhood Memories* (2013). He has also published widely on the history of bibliography and book collecting.